Moonshine *and* Salteens

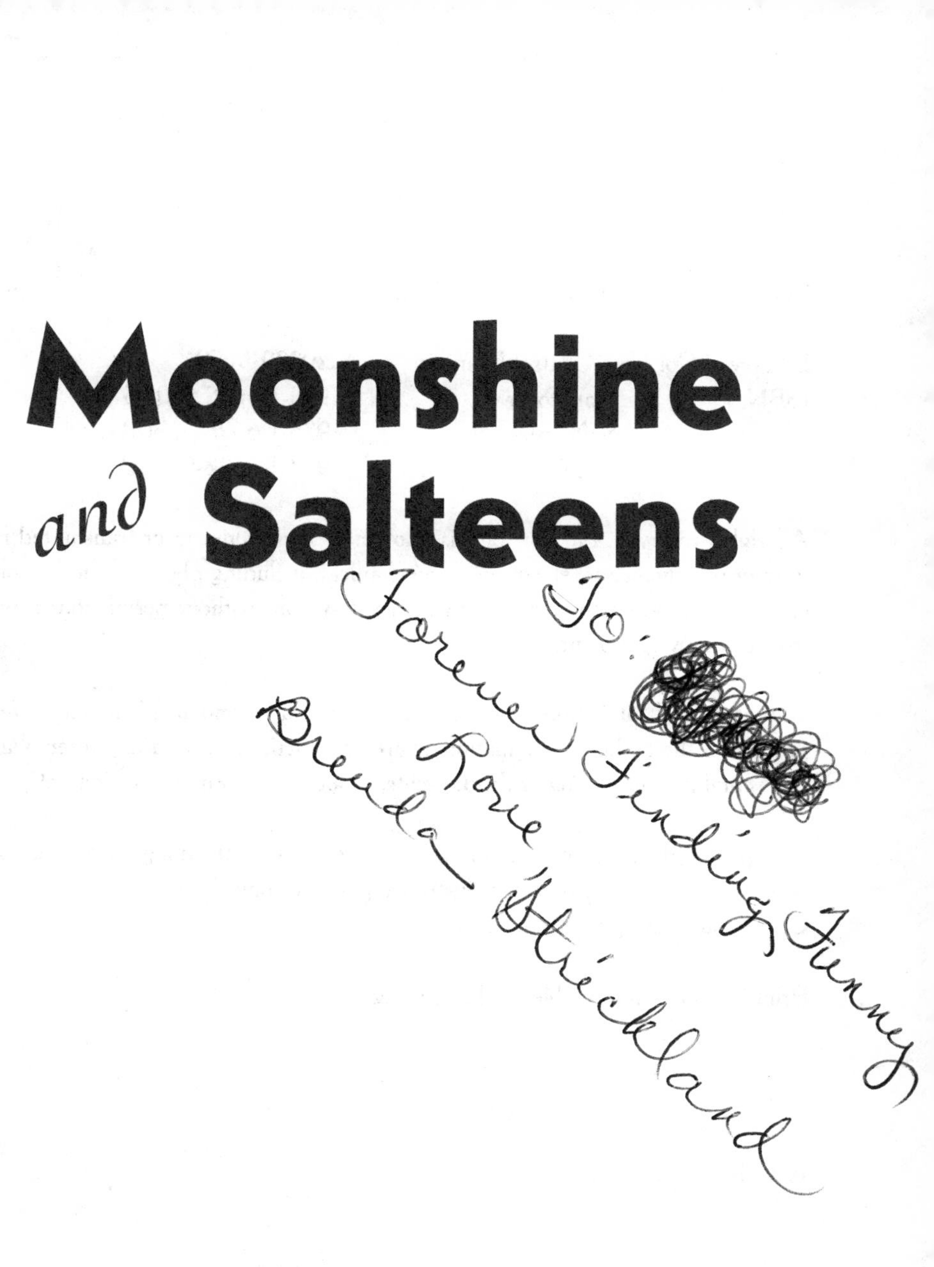

Moonshine *and* Salteens

Brenda Strickland

Library of Congress Control Number: 2022919679
ISBN: Hardcover 978-1-6698-5202-5
Softcover 978-1-6698-5201-8
eBook 978-1-6698-5203-2

Print information available on the last page.

Rev. date: 10/20/2022

To order additional copies of this book, contact:
Xlibris
844-714-8691
www.Xlibris.com
Orders@Xlibris.com
840967

As the proverb says, men cannot know each
other until they have eaten salt together.
—Aristotle

Prologue

I couldn't get the stick down in the sand dune! We had one member of our group, named Otis, who went to the movies or to dinner with us. He wouldn't come on any overnight trips like this vacation to Seaside Beach, so I had laminated a headshot of him and put it on a stick. We had already decided before we left that we were taking pictures of him with us as a gag wherever we went while we were here. This was going to be a picture of him like he was buried in the sand up to his neck.

I pulled the stick out because something was keeping it from going all the way down. I looked at the stick, and there was nothing on the end of it to keep it from going straight down. The sand in this dune was rather coarse and hard, but it shouldn't be this difficult to put a stick in it.

I could hear the seagulls squawking, children laughing and playing, and the waves crashing as I concentrated on my mission. There was a wide stretch of white sand going as far as I could see. My friends were already in position on the sand—tanning, reading books, putting on lotion, sipping cold drinks, and taking in the sights. There were only a few families on the beach, since school was back in session. Parents were watching their young children jumping waves. Some people were eating picnic lunches. I heard one man say to a woman, "Do you want to sit here or nearer the water?"

She replied, "We'd better sit here because the tide will start coming in soon."

I heard someone else say, "I'm going to have to bury my feet in the sand because they are red from my sunburn."

Jackie, our resident photographer, was ready to take a picture once I got Otis in position. She kept looking around with impatience, and I could tell that at any minute she was going to come up and start ramming the stick down in the sand for me. We had already taken a picture of Otis at the edge of the water and in the seagrass.

I gave it all the strength I had, but the stick still didn't budge. It was like there was a rock underneath, so I positioned the stick a few inches over in the sand and moved the stick back and forth as I burrowed down again. It still didn't want to go down all the way.

I pulled the stick out again as Jackie said, "For crying out loud." I looked down and saw something gold and shiny in the hole the stick had made. It looked like a woman's ring.

I said, "I see something down in the hole."

Jackie said, "Ooh, what is it? Maybe it's buried treasure!"

I dug down to where it was. I couldn't believe what I was seeing. I frantically started digging some more. I screamed.

I couldn't stop screaming. This was an off-the-charts, agonizing scream, and then I began to shake all over from shock. Jackie was the first one to come over and look. She said, "What is it? What's wrong?"

I said, "There's a hand in the sand." Then Jackie took a look, and she started screaming, too. By then, Kea had dropped her cold drink, Roberta her suntan lotion, and Lucy her book. All my girlfriends were there by my side.

Kea said, "Are you okay?"

I said breathlessly, "I'm better than the person in that sand dune."

Roberta said, "The dune doesn't look big enough to hold a dead body."

I said, "That's because I didn't see an arm or a body attached to the hand." Then all my girlfriends gasped in terror.

It seemed like everyone on the beach had heard me screaming, so a lot of people came running to satisfy their curiosity. Mothers were holding their young children back since it was potentially something they shouldn't see. People were pushing and weaving their way through the rubbernecking crowd. We had no control over the situation. Everyone was asking the same question. "What's going on?"

Someone looked in the hole and said, "Oh my God. There's a hand down there!"

Someone else said, "Is he or she dead?"

I said, "I would say that the odds are not in his or her favor that he or she is alive."

Word spread like wildfire. People ran up, found out what the chaos was about, fled the scene, and went to tell the rest of their party what was going on.

Lucy was an EMT, and her husband was a police officer, so she remained the calm one while the rest of us freaked out. Lucy yelled out, "It's time for all of us to step away and let the big boys do their job." She got out her phone and called 9-1-1. She used her expert speaking tone. "There's a DOA here on the beach near 101 Seaside Boulevard. Someone needs to come out here immediately to control the scene to make sure no evidence is disturbed. There is no need for resuscitation in this case." Lucy said to us, "They're sending a unit right away."

It was hot, and I felt faint. My mouth was dry, and I needed water. I drank my water, then Roberta's and Jackie's. I kept having random thoughts and talking crazy. "Who was that person in the sand? Why did I have to be the one to find the hand? I have ruined the vacation for all of you. I want to call my family. I need a hug. Jackie, this will be the last event you plan for us. Don't invite me anymore."

Jackie said, "Shirley Ann, you look at me. Calm down. This is not your fault."

We started hearing sirens. The crowd parted like the Red Sea, and I saw a whole posse of police coming toward us. Whenever I met a police car on the road, I slowed down, even if I knew I wasn't speeding, and at this very moment, I was thinking every irrational thought. I said, "Uh-oh! Are we in trouble?"

Chapter 1

Six Months Earlier

Oh no! I thought. Someone had thrown up in the women's bathroom again. I knew Jackie couldn't clean it up because if she saw it, she'd hurl. Kea, who had a very sensitive nose, couldn't stand the smell. No one else could leave his or her duties; therefore, I, Shirley Ann Dalton, a retired schoolteacher who had seen body fluids from every orifice every day of my educator's life, went into the bathroom.

We had all volunteered at a music venue in our spare time. It was a wonderful place to hear good music, but when someone decided to overdrink and throw up, it wasn't much fun to clean up. I'd never understood why anyone would pay fifty dollars for a ticket, drink before the show, drink the limit at the bar, and miss his or her favorite song by being sick in the bathroom.

All the volunteers at this music venue took their jobs seriously. The volunteer coordinator, named Arthur Murphy, had assigned our jobs. The positions changed a lot depending on the bands and the size of the crowd. Some of us checked people in. Others ushered people to their seats and guarded exit doors. Some volunteers were bartenders. Others helped with the catering for the bands.

All kinds of music were played at this venue. The crowds were different according to the type of band it was. If it was a '60s or '70s band, it was an older crowd, which meant they were calmer and didn't drink as much. If it was heavy metal or rock, then we would smell an occasional cannabis odor and see a lot of tie-dyed shirts. Most of the time, the crowds were very respectful, and we didn't have any trouble with anyone.

We all loved music, and that was the main reason we were here. It was a small venue that seated around four hundred people, which made it even better. Smaller venues had less open space for the music to travel, which led to a more powerful sound, and they could pack a lot more energy. The closer you were to the band, the more energy you could feel. The energy created a livelier crowd, and it gave everyone a more shared, connected, and enjoyable experience. This intimate experience gave people what we were all seeking—a connection. If you loved music, then you felt that connection.

If your volunteer job was checking people in, you were able to watch the show when the last person came through the door. If your job was as an usher or door guard, then you were in the auditorium where the music was playing. Bartenders were in another room. We got occasional breaks, but for the most part, we had to stay at our position the entire night. The hardest part for me was just standing there. If it was a good tune, I had to move my feet and dance a little. I don't know how some of the volunteers just stood there and didn't feel that beat and move. One of the volunteers named Nancy could not be still so we dubbed her "Dancy Nancy"!

After the show, some of us decided to go next door to a moonshine distillery when our duties were finished. The volunteers tried to leave positive vibes with the concertgoers after the show by bidding them farewell and telling them to come back, and we also cleaned up after the show, which consisted of picking up empty beer cans and other trash. I wasn't a big drinker, but I needed to wind down and socialize at the distillery before I hit the road to go home.

The distillery was an intimate building with a replica of an old-timey still in the back. There were pictures on the walls displaying the history of the moonshiners and their stills hidden in various places throughout the county we lived in. The distillery had mostly bar stools with a few tables scattered around the room. The back of the distillery looked like a living room, where we could sit and drink.

The kind and creative bartenders, Joni and Kim, had modernized the spirits by putting different flavors in the drinks to make them sellable and interesting. They infused the moonshine with fruit and added sparkling wine to make a delicious moonshine drink. They had one drink called "Scarlet Kiss" with raspberry liqueur and strawberry moonshine. Another one, called "Better than Sex," had pineapple-infused moonshine, coconut cream, and vanilla pudding. "Get Lucky" was another drink sold near St. Patrick's Day with the rim rolled in Lucky Charms cereal. The presentation was always beautiful with garnishes, and the glass rims were always rolled in some type of sugar or something interesting.

The guy who owned this distillery had gotten his liquor recipe from his relatives, who used to make it illegally. He wore bib overalls to make the distillery look more authentic and also because they were comfortable. His daughter worked there and was a great asset. She was there for any job including public relations, while her daddy was in charge of production.

We all lived in a little town in the south, where the claim to fame was making good moonshine. The locals still talked about one of the longest trials in Virginia's history in 1935. Then certain lawmen had gotten a lot of bribery money from bootleggers. There had been nearly four hundred witnesses and over fifty days of testimony, and the jury had convicted several people, including federal agents, for bribery connected to the illegal sale of moonshine.

Five women and one man were sitting at our table at the distillery. We were all laughing and having a good time. Otis, our man friend, loved music and getting pictures and autographs of celebrities. He had dozens of albums in his collection. He always kept us laughing.

I had known Jackie before the venue opened. We had lived in the same town in our earlier years. Jackie loved to go and do things all the time. Her birthday was in October, and she celebrated during the whole month. She traveled a lot, did snow skiing in the winter, and went boating in the summer. She loved to party and socialize and was a very giving person. She took pictures everywhere she went. She should have been an event planner.

Kea was the life of the party. She could come up with some great one-liners. She loved her family and was a doting grandmother. She also loved to sit in the sun and go boating. She didn't like scary things, and she was also a super smeller. She could tell you exactly what a smell was if you couldn't figure it out.

Lucy was our technology expert. She loved camping and kayaking. She volunteered at a local rescue squad and was an active grandparent.

Roberta was a retired psychiatric nurse. She had long, flowing hair and wore loose clothes. She was our resident hippie. She was the calm in every storm. Her favorite thing was to go to art museums, and she also loved history. She and Otis were the singles in our group, though Otis claimed he was secretly married to a certain country music star.

As I mentioned earlier, I was a retired educator. I loved to cook. I had even catered for some of the bands at the music venue. One thing my friends and I all had in common was our love for music and the arts.

All the women in our group liked to do different arts and crafts of some sort. Roberta was our painter. Jackie was the maker of pottery. Kea was the quilter. Robin did several crafts, but she was known for making things on her cutting machine, such as attaching iron-on decals to T-shirts or sticking vinyl cutouts on cups and glasses.

I loved to crochet and knit. I could tie a knot in everything. I liked to make things for my granddaughter. I had made her a turtle costume, a mermaid costume, a tutu, and many other things. Now she let me do these things because she was too young to know better. One day she was going to grow up and be like the reluctant Ralphie in the movie *A Christmas Story*, whose mom made him wear a bunny costume his aunt had made. My granddaughter was going to tell her parents when she got older, "Don't make me wear what Granny made me!"

Jackie suggested that we all go to the salt cave the next day. This was our first adventure together. It was relaxing and a lot of fun. The salt cave was a man-made, spa-like place that had salt vapors in the air, and most of these places had salt bricks on the walls, stalactite ceilings made of salt, and crushed salt on the floor. They played soft, elevator music, and the place was supposed to be relaxing. We wouldn't know because we are too busy gossiping and laughing. Breathing the salt vapors was supposed to be a healthy thing to do, like breathing the salt air at the beach, and we enjoyed going just to socialize.

I had struggled since I retired from teaching to find my place in this world. Before retirement, I'd had no time for anything except my family and work. I needed a place to belong. I'd tried being on the board of different organizations. I'd been in a few community theater plays, which I really enjoyed. My favorite role was Quiser Boudreaux, the cursing curmudgeon, in *Steel Magnolias*. Learning a lot of lines and the time it took to rehearse could be very stressful, but the role was fulfilling. I was a very curious person and loved to people watch. I helped to research and write a play for a moonshine festival held in the community. I loved the theater and history, so this was a delightful project. I enjoyed participating in community projects. I felt like I was helping myself and others around me.

I was a social person for the most part. I needed healthy relationships to feel happy. Research tells us that these connections are healthy for our minds and bodies. It's good for our blood pressure, strengthens our immune systems, and leads to longer and more fulfilled lives. However, after the age of twenty, it became hard to make new friends because my life (career and family) got in the way. Until I volunteered at the music venue, I didn't have a close set of girlfriends. I felt the place for me was the music venue, and now I felt like I had a new circle of friends to which I belonged.

The next week we went to the salt cave again without Otis and invited another person named Kathy to go with us. Kea planned it so when we went into the cave, we started taking our clothes off, like we had to be nude to do this activity. We showed Kathy where to put her shoes, because we had to put socks on before we went into the cave. After we got in, all of us but poor Kathy started unbuttoning our tops.

Kathy said, "Y'all didn't tell me you had to be naked to do this. I don't want to take my clothes off." She started walking toward the door. We all laughed hysterically and started buttoning our shirts.

"Come on back in here," Roberta said. "We were just messing with you!" Kathy came back in, and we all lay back in these cushy lounging chairs.

I crossed my legs, pointed my hands toward the ceiling, and began to hum a yoga mantra, which to Kathy probably looked like a witches' coven moment. All the other girls joined in. "Mmmmm. Mmmmm."

Kathy looked at all of us like we were crazy and then said, "Mmmmmm. I get it now. You are trying to fool me again."

Kea said, "Thank you for being such a good sport. It wasn't my idea. I wouldn't dare treat anybody like that." That made us all laugh harder.

Lucy said, "Y'all are crazy, and I love it!"

Jackie said, "We ought to all go on an overnight trip somewhere. What do you like to do?"

Kea said, "I love the sun and the beach. Let's go somewhere and really have some fun. Just remember that if we go to the movies while we're gone, I don't do scary."

Roberta said, "I don't care. I just love to go anywhere. I don't mind driving at all. Let me know if there is anything I can bring or do before we go."

I said, "I love the beach. I'll cook some wherever we go. I am a foodie, so I do want to go to some good restaurants."

Kea said, "I want to go to a restaurant that serves crab legs."

Lucy said, "I also love crab legs. I love the beach and mountains. I'll make us some T-shirts for our trip."

Kea said, "We need to call ourselves 'the Salteens' since we love coming to the salt cave and going to the beach."

I said, "And we are all older teenagers at heart."

Jackie said, "I will plan the beach trip."

The next week we had a "Bye, Bye, Boobie" party for Lucy. She was having a breast reduction due to back pain and other issues. Our friendship was established enough now so we all came running whenever one of us had something major going on in his or her life. We met at the Moonshine Distillery for the "Bye, Bye, Boobie" party. Jackie called the distillery and asked permission for us to bring food since they served only snacks like pretzels and peanuts. Kea always brought gluten-free food since she couldn't have any other options.

I brought a cup in the shape of a breast. That was Lucy's sippy cup for the night. We toasted Lucy and wished her the best. She ended up having ten pounds of her breasts removed. Until she was back on her feet, we fixed food for her and her husband and helped her all we could. As soon as she healed, we planned our beach trip.

Chapter 2

We decided to go to Seaside Beach. From the pictures, it seemed to have jaw-dropping beauty, lots of nature, and no big-box stores. This area was famous for music festivals. We thought this place would be ideal since we all loved music. We waited until peak season was over so the beach wouldn't be as crowded and the apartment rates would be cheaper. At this time of year, the area would still have gorgeous weather but not be quite as hot. The weather was still good enough to sit on the beach and enjoy the golden sun, dazzling sand, and the ocean. I really didn't like to go anywhere if it was like a sauna. The main draw would be the peaceful beach, where we would search for rare seashells. We could enjoy the serenity of the wind blowing lightly and the frothy waves crashing. After all, "girls just wanna have sun"!

Jackie got us an apartment to rent. We needed two cars so we would have room for five suitcases and wouldn't feel crowded on the long drive. We could all ride in one car while we were down there. Also, not all of us might want to go to the same places all the time during our stay. Lucy and Kea were our drivers, and after we decided who was going to ride with whom during the five-hour drive, we were all set. Lucy was an expert on a craft-cutting machine, and she made us all T-shirts to wear. People loved those shirts, and they stopped us to see what they said.

Mine said, "I'll bring the bail money." Jackie's said, "I'll bring the alcohol." Roberta's said, "I'll bring the voice of reason." Kea's said, "I'll bring the getaway car," and Lucy's said, "I'll bring the bad decisions."

We arrived at the beach near sunset. The plethora of windows and the balcony in our apartment gave us what we needed: a wonderful view of the ocean. The colors of the horizon were a perfect rainbow today. There was nothing like the smell of the salt air; the calming, rhythmic sound of the waves; and the swirling cries of the seagulls to put us in a happy place in our hearts and souls.

We all needed to settle in, unpack, and call our families to tell them we had arrived. Then we wanted to go down and put our feet in the sand. I loved the feel of the warm sand on my feet. We packed our beach bags with towels, water, and snacks. I also put Otis's laminated head picture on a stick in my bag. We were all so excited to finally be here. This was our chance to relax and have some fun.

As we walked down near the ocean, we had to use our foot muscles to push up out of the sand, because we had sunk way down.

Kea said, "We look like penguins waddling instead of sophisticated women who are on vacation." We all laughed. We laid our towels in the sand. Then Jackie and I decided to take some pictures of Otis. I took him out of my beach bag, Jackie got out her camera, and we headed toward the sand dune behind us. We took several pictures before we got to the sand dune.

That was when we made the shocking discovery.

Finding a hand in the sand during our first day at the beach wasn't on our vacation agenda. This wasn't how we'd wanted to spend our weekend at the beach. After Lucy shooed all the rubberneckers away from the scene of the obvious crime and chaos settled down somewhat, we plopped down on the beach without any regard for the sand gathering in unknown places. We were simply trying to recover from seeing the hand in the sand dune.

I was still swooning from the experience. A kind police officer, named Zach, walked up to me and tried to get me to focus. He wanted to talk to all "the Salteens" individually. He asked me a lot of questions, including, "Why were you at the sand dune?"

I said, "To take a picture of our friend Otis on a stick in the sand." I'm sure he thought I was delirious at that point. To prove I still had some faculties left, I showed him Otis.

He said, "How did you find the hand?"

"I found it when Otis's stick wouldn't go all the way down in the sand." Now he could interpret my statement in so many ways, but Zach kept a straight face.

"Who was with you?" This young policeman had a very soothing voice.

I replied, "All of my girlfriends and half of the beach came to see what was going on."

"When did all of you come to the beach?" Zach asked.

"We just got here today and unpacked," I said in a frustrated tone.

"How long are you going to stay?" Zach asked.

"Just for the weekend." I was beginning to wonder whether he thought one of us had done this terrible thing.

"Where are you staying?" Zach asked.

"In Seaside Apartments behind the sand dune."

He got up to leave, then asked, "Can I have Otis, please?"

"Huh?" I said.

"Can I have the picture on the stick? It may have evidence on it," he said. I reluctantly gave Otis to him.

I guess he could tell I was just about spent, so he stopped asking questions. He also wanted to know my phone number and whether I would be available later for questioning. He gave me his card with his phone number on it. He asked the rest of my friends similar questions. Zach had dark, penetrating eyes and a demeanor that would make anyone confess to anything whether he or she did it or not.

People were coming from everywhere to find out what was going on. A young man came running up to us and said, "What happened? My name is David, and I manage the gas station behind here. I saw all of the police cars go by and heard the sirens. Then I saw a crowd here. I thought at first someone had drowned. I knew it had to be something serious."

Pointing behind me, because I still couldn't look back there, I told him, "I found a hand in that sand dune."

"What? Was it just a hand? It wasn't a whole body?"

"Yes. It was only a hand." I could tell he was visibly upset. He had a worried look on his face while running his hands through his hair and began to pace back and forth in the sand. He had grease all over his hands. I wouldn't be putting them in my hair, but he must not be as high maintenance as I was. He probably hadn't taken the time to clean them well after working on a car engine and had just come running down to see what was going on.

David said, "Do they know who it is?" I couldn't tell whether he was worried that it might be someone he knew or whether he thought the incident would be bad for his business, since it was right behind the crime scene.

I wanted to say that most people couldn't tell who someone was by his or her hand but stopped myself. At least, I had a little tact left in me. "I assume that forensics will answer that question for all of us," I said. David left and tried to talk to the police. I was sure they wouldn't tell him anything.

David came back over and looked me in the eye with kindness. I could smell his cologne, a woodsy, outdoor smell. He said, "If y'all need to talk or need anything during your stay, please let me know. I know this has got to be tough on you. You come down here to unwind and have a good time, and something this horrendous happens." He looked up and saw someone walking toward us. He looked rather disgusted and in a different tone said, "I gotta go."

Next, a rather tall, dark, and handsome man came up to us and wanted to shake our hands. I guess he didn't know I had been an inch away from touching a dead hand. He said, "Hi, my name is George Anderson. I'm the mayor of Seaside Beach. I just heard the news. I hope this situation won't ruin your stay. I'm so sorry about all of this."

I said, "Our trip is already ruined." I guess George didn't know what to say, so he left.

That was really nice of David and the mayor to say all those things, but by then I had become suspicious of everyone around us.

The next person who came by to talk was a different story. I turned to my friends and said, "Here's a word of advice. You're going to see a whole lot more than you'll ever want to see in just a second." It was an elderly man with a very dark suntan and very saggy skin wearing a very tiny bathing suit. I was thinking he was a local who wanted to find out what was going on. Evidently, he hadn't heard the news.

Instead, he came up and wanted a woman. He asked, "Do you ladies like what is in my banana hammock?"

I said, "They are nice Fruit of the Looms, but there's more fruit than looms!" We were all laughing hysterically at him, but I think he thought we were laughing with him. I'm sure people were wondering how we could laugh at a time like this, but I seemed to laugh inappropriately whenever I got in an uncomfortable situation. This man was playing music on his phone, and believe it or not, the song was "Let's Get It On!"

"Would you ladies like to smell my belly? I just rubbed some coconut suntan oil on myself."

That was our cue to leave. We were kicking up some sand to get away from him. I had to go down the beach and go the long way to our apartment. There was no way I could go by where the hand was. The police had tape around the crime scene now, but I still couldn't even look in that direction.

Chapter 3

After we got ourselves somewhat together, we went back to the apartment to rewind. My legs were so wobbly that I could hardly make it back on my own. I locked and double-checked all the windows and doors. I heard Lucy sniffle, and then we all started crying. Lucy was always the one who cried first because her heart was so open. She volunteered for a lot of organizations. You would think she would be the cold, nerdy sort since she was brilliant at computers, but she wasn't.

I went to the bathroom and scrubbed my hands until they were red. Although I didn't think I had touched the dead hand, I wanted to get any possible cooties from it off me. I then went to my room to process what had just happened and needed some time alone. I leaned against the wall, slowly crept down to the floor, and cried some more. I called my husband and son and told them what had happened and how much I loved them. I had my cry, and now I was getting angry.

I had an insatiable curiosity. Who could have done something that awful? Why hadn't the person put the hand in the ocean and not where any person or animal could find it? I was ready for action. If I saw that a person has been wronged, I wasn't one to let the evildoers get by with it.

I came out of my room, and everyone's eyes were on me. I guess they wanted to make sure I hadn't had a complete breakdown. Roberta was a former psychiatric nurse. I guessed she would be the first to diagnose my issue.

Lucy asked, "Are you okay?"

I said, "Yes, but I need to ask all of you a question. I know most people wouldn't want to get involved, but I can't stand it. Could you stay a while longer if needed?"

"Why?" Jackie asked.

"I have to find out what happened. I can't leave without knowing who that hand belonged to and who did this to him or her. As I get older, I have found out that if you don't paddle your own kayak, you don't move." I waited for the roll call.

Kea said, "Yes, but I don't do scary."

I said, "I will try my best to keep us out of danger."

Lucy said, "Yes, I want to help."

Roberta said, "Yes."

Jackie said, "Yes."

She called the rental agency and extended our stay. I was ready to play amateur detective. All of us were retired, so we could all stay until we ran out of money. We had all allocated a certain amount of money to spend on this trip. Since we were retired and on fixed incomes, we had to stay within a budget.

I said, "Roberta, I am so sorry for ruining this for you. Your mama just died, and this was an opportunity for you to forget about all of the sadness. Instead, I have created madness."

Roberta said, "Shirley Ann, you know this is not your fault."

Jackie got out some moonshine, and we had a little toast to Roberta's mother.

"I have an idea. People like to talk, especially drunk talk, so let's go to a bar tonight," Kea said, and she explained her plan. "Let's go as a bridal party. Who wants to be the bride?"

Roberta volunteered since she was the only single one in the group. It was getting late, so we hurriedly went to the party store in a nearby town before it closed and bought a mock bridal veil and some sashes that said "Bride to Be" and "Bridesmaid." Kea was a quilter and an excellent seamstress. She could have done a better job at making the bridal supplies. She bought more net tulle for our veils to make us look a little more authentic.

Lucy asked the clerk at the party store, "What bars do the locals hang out at?"

She replied, "The Bay Bar is probably the most popular bar for everyone around here."

We went to a print shop. I downloaded a new photo of Otis from social media and had a new "innocent Otis" picture created since the "guilty Otis" was in police custody. We had him laminated, and then we taped him to a stick.

We headed home and ate a few snacks we had brought with us. None of us felt like eating a meal because of what had happened earlier that day. Later that night, we all piled into one car and went to The Bay Bar. We were ready and excited about our first plan.

We decided to separate once we got to the bar so we could meet with more people, and we would talk about what we had learned after we got back to our apartment.

We were older women, so we couldn't depend on our young, spry bodies and cleavage to get people to talk, so the bridal party idea was a great strategy. Also, we could rely on our great personalities to find out information.

People clapped when we walked in and wound our way through the bar, waving at folks. We found prime seats, and the bartender gave us free drinks. We knew we wouldn't be in those seats for a long time. We all felt like getting drunker than ever after what had happened to us, but we were specifically there on a mission, so we made our rounds, talking to as many people as possible. It was hard to hear because the band was playing loud, but I did hear Kea tell a group that she was the flower girl.

Someone I talked to had one too many drinks. Looking at me with squinty eyes and obnoxious breath, he said, "I'm going to a clance dub. Wanna come?" I finally figured out he was asking me to join him at a dance club. That would be a no from me.

I overheard another overdrinker say, "That's when I found out that son of a gun was sleeping with my wife." I wondered if he would have told that story if he were sober.

We had someone take our picture with Otis. After a while, we conferred and realized we had gotten all we could out of this occasion, and we were all exhausted, so we left.

At the apartment, most of us agreed that we hadn't heard anything that would help our investigation. Kea and I talked only to tourists who hadn't heard about the incident. Lucy and Jackie talked to some local people, but either they weren't talking, or they didn't know anything about the hand. Roberta said, "The guy I talked to seemed to think the death was drug related. He said there was a lot of that going on in the particular area where we were staying."

That was a clue, but we needed names and a connection. We also needed to find out whose hand had been found in that sand dune. I made sure all the doors and windows were locked and actually went to bed with my clothes on. I really needed to snuggle under the covers with my husband for comfort tonight.

Chapter 4

I bolted upright in my bed the next morning, my heart hammering in my chest. The moonshine I had drunk last night was burning my throat and threatening to come up. I had a nightmare about what had happened yesterday. My head was pounding from what I assumed were stress and anxiety. I knew it wasn't a hangover because I wasn't a big drinker, and last night I had wanted to be aware of my surroundings and get as much information as I could.

I finally got dressed and went into the living room. I looked out at the beautiful ocean. People were walking up and down the beach like nothing unusual had happened yesterday.

After everyone got up and was ready, we discussed a new plan of action since last night had been a bust. I said, "What do you think we need to do today?"

Roberta said, "I really don't want to go to the beach and sit around. We need to get some good information."

Lucy said, "Why don't we go into town and see what the locals say about what happened? Then maybe tonight we will be ready to have some fun at a nightclub or something." We all got into one car and drove into town.

Seaside Beach had old-school charm. There were lots of cottages in pastel candy colors with tiled roofs and stucco. There was a lovely main street running parallel to the sound. There were mostly little boutiques selling beach souvenirs. Beach music was playing on loudspeakers. I heard "Be Young, Be Foolish, Be Happy" by the Tams, "My Girl" by the Temptations, and "Under the Boardwalk" by the Drifters.

A lot of the shop owners were putting out their open signs when we arrived. We were trying to beat the heat by going early. Some of the shop owners were putting out dog bowls full of fresh water, since a lot of people walked their dogs down the boardwalk. A man was walking up and down the street, shaking hands, and hugging people.

Lucy stopped. "Oh no. I hate politicians!"

I said, "I couldn't agree more."

Kea said, "Let's avoid him like the plague. Here's a ladies' clothing store. He has no reason to go in here." We all made a beeline for that shop and tried to hurriedly sneak away. We huddled in a corner and giggled while the store owner had a puzzled look on her face. The mayor must have seen us. He caught us and came right into the shop. We had a deer-in-the-headlights look as he walked in.

He reached out to shake our hands, a gesture not one of us responded to, and said, "It is so nice to see you again. I hope you are enjoying our little town."

Jackie said, "It's beautiful here. The town has so much charm. We came down mainly to ask if anybody knew anything about what happened yesterday. We can't get it off of our minds."

The mayor hesitated. "Forget about that. Go shopping. Go on an excursion. Enjoy the beach." He opened the door and walked off.

"My goodness, he's everywhere," Kea whispered.

The ladies' shop owner walked up to us and said, "Our mayor is the best. He loves promoting our little town."

Lucy responded, "I could tell he really wants us to think positive about Seaside. I can't blame him for that."

Most of the shop owners said the police had already questioned them. Here we were, complete strangers asking questions, so we told them why we were interested in the hand after we had introduced ourselves, thinking it would help us get information. Most of them just shook their heads and couldn't believe what had happened. They ended up asking us more questions than we did. The shop owners were curious about where we had come from and what we had seen.

We opened the door to one place, Seaside Shop, and a bell rang above our heads. The shelves were packed with Seaside Beach logo T-shirts and other souvenirs. Two young men walked toward us from the back of the store, looking rather sheepishly. I guess they knew we had caught them. I didn't need Kea's nose to tell what they had been doing. A marijuana odor wafted from the back. They were dressed rather casually, but that was okay in a beach town. They both had long hair in ponytails. One of them, whose name tag said "Oliver," came up to us and asked, "Hi, may I help you?"

"Yes," I said, "we were wondering if you know anything about what happened at the beach yesterday. We are the ones who found the hand, and we are really upset and want to know more about it. We were wondering if you know of, or have seen, any suspicious activity going on lately."

Both men looked at each other. The guy whose name tag said "John" started shuffling his feet and clearing his throat. He seemed to be very nervous and acting weird. He never said a word.

Oliver said, "The police have already been in here. We heard about it, but that's all we can tell you. We don't know any details or have any helpful information. I'm sorry. Have a nice day." He rapidly dismissed us, and they both turned their backs to us and started absent-mindedly folding T-shirts. Of course, I was sure five strange women walking into their place of business and asking questions weren't what they were used to. We left the shop after that.

These two men had acted a bit strangely. The guy named John had squinty eyes and was scratching himself. My son was a drug counselor, and I knew the signs of drug use. Marijuana was now legal. As long as that was all that this young man was doing, then he would be okay. I remembered the comment from The Bay Bar that the murder could be drug related.

"Well, that was awkward," Roberta said. "I wonder if they were nervous about us smelling the weed or if they really know something."

I said, "We need to get a few groceries while we're here. We can't get many because there isn't enough room in the car for a lot."

We picked up a few essentials. We had planned on eating breakfast and lunch at the apartment and going out to eat at night.

None of us could just let what had happened the day before go. Jackie said, "Let's go by the Seaside Oil Company, that gas station the young man named David manages."

"Who?" I said.

Roberta said, "He was the one who came running down to the beach to see what was going on yesterday."

"Oh yes," I said. "I was so out of it that I forgot about him."

We pulled into the service station and got out. David had only one customer, and he immediately recognized us and came right over. "Hi, how are y'all doing today?" he said. "Have you heard any news?" He seemed to be very kind and sincere.

Lucy said, "We were hoping you could help us. Have you heard anything about the hand? Do you know how all of this could have happened?"

He shook his head and said, "I have no idea. We are a small town with very little crime. Every now and then, a tourist will get drunk and get into trouble. I wonder if someone came here from somewhere else and did this, because I can't imagine anyone that I know is capable of this, and I know everyone in town."

Jackie said, "Let us know if you hear anything. We plan to go to a nightclub and dance tonight around eight o'clock. We need to get rid of some of our tension. Do you know of a good place?"

He said, "The best dance music and dance floor are at the Full Moon Party Club."

Lucy asked, "Does Seaside Beach have Uber drivers? We've never used their services before. Our little town doesn't have Uber, but I figure a tourist town would have to have it."

"Yes, we do," he said. He looked around, pointed to a man standing near us, and said, "I need to see what he wants." We left and went back to our apartment.

"Did you notice the man with his back to us at the service station?" Jackie said. "He was trying to eavesdrop on us. He was listening to every word of our conversation. I guess if he is from the town that he wanted to know what was going on, but why didn't he just come over and talk to us?" We all had seen him, but we had been focused on David and what he had to say.

Roberta said, "David certainly seems to be a nice young man."

I finally called Zach, the kind young police officer who had questioned us the day before. "This is Officer Zach," he said.

"Hello," I said. "This is Shirley Ann Dalton, the lady who found the hand in the sand. Do you know who the hand belonged to? Have the police found the rest of the person? Have you found the murder weapon, and do you have any suspects?"

Zach said, "Whoa! Whoa! You're going too fast! Even if I did know any of this information, I couldn't tell you. I *can* tell you that we don't have much to go on right now. I understand that you are upset about everything, but I promise you that I will try my best to get to the bottom of this."

I said, "I'm sorry to bother you, but I won't rest until I know what happened to that person."

Zach said, "I feel the same way." I could tell he didn't want to talk and was very preoccupied with the case. He got a tone with me like I was being nosy, so I let it go.

Late afternoon around dinnertime, there was a knock on the door. It was David. "I found out from my friend Zach where y'all were staying. I told my mom what had happened to you, and she made you something to eat."

Kea asked, "Do you still live with your mom?"

He replied, "Yes, I used all of my money to buy the business, and my mom said I could stay with her as long as I needed. My dad died last year, so I help her with the yard work and any heavy labor that needs to be done around the house."

I said, "You look about the age of my son."

David said, "I am thirty-eight years old. I went to college and majored in auto mechanics. All I ever wanted to do was play with car engines, so when the opportunity came around for me to buy the service station, I did it. I'm not married, so I have saved a lot of money. It took a lot to buy the business. I even bought the vacant lots on either side of it in case I want to expand one day."

Before David left, we asked him to thank his mom for us for the food, and then we chowed down. We had to save money any way we could, so this food was great since we didn't have to pay for groceries to eat in or for a restaurant if we went out to eat.

Chapter 5

That night we decided to get away from that area of the beach and go inland to the nightclub David had recommended. We thought a little dancing might lift our spirits. No one wanted to drive, so we called a driver. The driver got there early, and we asked the question we were supposed to, based on our order information. "Are you Michael?" Jackie said.

He said, "No, I'm Art. Michael got called on another job, and they sent me." We climbed in, and I noticed the blue van hadn't exactly been cleaned up for passengers. He wore a hat down low on his head, and we could barely see his face. He wasn't dressed for the job either. He also looked strangely familiar to me, but I had met so many people over the last few days, and I was beginning to get overloaded.

Art immediately started asking us questions. "What have y'all been doing since you got here?"

Kea answered, "We are the people who discovered the 'hand in the sand,' as we heard the media is now calling the horrible incident."

He said, "Did y'all see the body?"

Kea said, "No, just a hand. We don't know if the police discovered the body or not. I guess that's why the media called it the 'hand in the sand,' because that's all anyone saw."

Then he said, "I heard you have been asking all kinds of questions in our little town. Why are y'all doing that?"

"We are upset and want to help find out anything we can," I said, trying not to sound irritated.

Then he asked, "What did the mayor have to say about the situation?"

"Nothing," Roberta said. "He was being a politician, promoting himself and preventing any negativity from being connected to the area."

Roberta and I exchanged glances. She group-texted all of us. She said she had told her friend about us taking an Uber. Her friend had said to make sure the driver had an Uber sticker on the car's windshield. We looked and didn't see one. I took a deep breath and said, "Where is your Uber sticker?"

Art hesitated and replied, "Uh. Uh. My other car with the sticker on it is being repaired." He started driving erratically with an angry look on his face. Kea even screamed when he went around a curve too fast. He looked at her and said, "What's wrong with you?"

Art seemed to know a lot about what was going on with us, more than he should, and I was getting uncomfortable. We had all known to ask for Michael, and this wasn't him. I thought Uber should have called us if they switched drivers. His van didn't have a sticker with their logo on it. It was okay for us to ask questions but not for others to ask us questions. I began to get suspicious of him.

I said, "Can you stop at the next place that has a public restroom, please?" My friends looked at me strangely because they knew I had just gone to the bathroom before we got in the car. I nonchalantly texted everyone, "GET OUT OF THIS VAN AS SOON AS HE STOPS." Art stopped, and we ran away from the car as fast as we could.

Through the open window, he yelled at us, "Mind your own business. It's not your monkeys or your circus!" He didn't ask for money or anything.

We were very upset and stuck at a convenience store. We didn't even know what the address was. My knees were shaking. We didn't have a vehicle, so Jackie called the Uber company. Her voice was shaking as she said, "We are the group you picked up at 101 Seaside Boulevard. A guy named Art picked us up. We weren't comfortable with him and asked him to drop us off. She looked around at the sign on the convenience store. We are at the Gretna Minute Market. Do you know where that is?" She listened for a while and said, "I see. You don't have to worry. We have learned our lesson. Can someone pick us up here and take us to our destination? Thank you."

When she got off the phone, she said, "Michael did come to the address of our rental apartment, but we weren't there. They told me not to ever get in the car with anyone unless it had their business logo sticker on the windshield, and they would call us if they changed drivers. Our driver's name is Jamison. Michael is busy driving someone else." We realized how ignorant we were of this whole situation.

A vehicle drove into the Gretna Minute Market. It had the business logo in the window. Jackie asked, "What is your name?"

The driver said, "My name is Jamison."

We were nervous now about whom we rode with, so Kea said, "I just got out, and I'm on my meds now, so I should be okay on this ride." It took all we had to keep from laughing hysterically. We were still nervous.

"We trust you, honey. We know you're just fine now. You learned your lesson," Roberta said.

Jackie joined in, "It's okay. Anybody can make a mistake." The driver looked perplexed and somewhat scared. I knew he couldn't wait to get rid of us.

We went to the nightclub for a little while, but we weren't in the mood to be there after what had happened with scary Art. We danced to a few good songs. Normally, we are always up for a good dance party. I was beginning to wonder what we had gotten ourselves into. I went up to Kea and said, "You are being very brave. I know you don't do scary."

Kea said, "I'm beginning to think we are all crazy."

Roberta said, "I know we are in a small beach town, but how on earth was that guy named Art aware of everything we have done?" We all looked at each other and shrugged. We did take a picture of the head of Otis dancing with all of us.

When the driver picked us up, we noticed that it was the same guy named Jamison. Jackie said, "I'm surprised that you came back and picked us up."

He said, "This is a small town, so it is only Michael and me who do this in the off-season. During the summer, we have more drivers."

Lucy said, "You know we made up the whole 'crazy scene' just to mess with you. We got scared of the previous driver. I guess you heard that he wasn't from your company."

He laughed and said, "I heard about what happened to you guys. When you got in and started talking the scary stuff, I was beginning to wonder if you had made up the story about the previous driver. I was skeptical about even picking you up again. I'm glad you told me you were kidding about what you said earlier."

Then we all had a good laugh about it. When we got back to the apartment, we paid Jamison generously for putting up with us.

I called the police as soon as we got into the apartment. I was so glad Zach was there. I needed to tell him about the guy named Art in the blue van who had picked us up and warned us to mind our own business.

Zach said, "I was told by some of the people in town that you were asking them questions. That could be really dangerous. Let the police do their jobs. Now that I've finished fussing at you, give me all of the details on this Art guy."

I told him every detail I could think of. "He was in an old, messy blue van, and he was dressed very sloppy. He had a hat pulled down low on his face so we couldn't get a good look at him. He looked to be about fifty years old. He looked familiar to me, but I can't imagine where I have seen him."

Zach said, "I'll look into it, but I am overwhelmed with this other case."

I hung up my phone and told the others, "I called Zach and told him about Art in the blue van, and he gave me a butt chewing about asking questions around town. I think he is worried about us."

Roberta said, "I think you're right. He *is* worried about us."

Kea said, "I'm worried about us, too. Let's go to bed and start fresh in the morning." We called it a night.

All of us crawled into one bed together and discussed our next move, and we came up with zilch.

We decided to take a picture of Otis in the bed with all of us. Otis had a strong Christian faith. We didn't want him to be offended by our taking the picture. He was laughing when we called him after we sent the picture to him. We put him on speaker so we could all talk to him. He knew we meant no harm and were full of shenanigans. I said, "You won't believe this, but I found a hand in the sand when we first got down here." He laughed at first until he realized I wasn't kidding.

"You are serious?" he said.

Kea said, "I'm afraid she is. You know how Shirley Ann is. She kept digging into that sand dune when your picture wouldn't go down in there. She found out that the hand was preventing the stick from going down. She is very curious and won't let things go. We have tried to find out anything to help solve this case but have had no luck so far."

Otis said, "You mean my picture has touched a dead hand?"

I said, "I'm afraid so, and you are in police custody right now. I can't leave until I know what happened to that poor person."

He said, "I wish I could be down there with you for support and to give all of you a big hug. In all the books I have ever read, the first suspect is the spouse. Do you know anything about him or her?"

Jackie said, "We know nothing. We don't know who it is or if the person is married, so the police can't accuse the spouse."

Lucy changed the subject and asked, "Whose autograph did you get this week? We know how you love it."

Otis said excitedly, "Chrissy Metz, Guy Fieri, and Carrie Underwood."

We all said, "Ooh." He had received several autographs in the mail. He was going to a big event in Nashville in a few days to get more. We hung up and then had our typical shot of moonshine before going to our bedrooms.

Chapter 6

We went to the beach the next day because we couldn't figure out what to do next. We just lay on the beach, thinking we could get a good vibe with the high tide. The shimmering ocean waves were so soothing, and it looked like a blue mirror from the rays of the hot sun. It was a marvelous view, and we were having fun, especially Kea, who loved to sunbathe. I loved to sit in a low chair at the edge of the water and stick my feet in to keep myself cool and read a good book. After a while, I was getting too much sun, so I joined the others under an umbrella.

Then suddenly, four men sat very close to where we were sitting. They were middle-aged men who seemed to look decent enough. They all pulled beers out of a cooler and began drinking. There was plenty of room on the beach. This beach was never that crowded unless they were having a music festival. The men seemed to want to listen to anything we had to say and stared at us the whole time. One or two of them nodded at us when they sat down, but they never tried to talk to us. This seemed very strange. Why were they crowding us?

A helicopter passed over us, and Kea put down her magazine, looking up at the sky with her hand shading her eyes. She said, "Is that the paparazzi following us again?" We all knew what to do and chimed in.

"Yes, I told our agent to get them off of our backs while we were on break from touring. We're trying to relax here," Lucy said. She got out some water from the cooler.

"What day is our next gig?" Jackie said.

The men kept giving each other puzzled looks.

"I don't know. I would have to look on our calendar to know for sure," Roberta said. She dug down in her beach bag to find her calendar on her phone. She pretended to look at her calendar. "Our next gig is not until next month. Shirley Ann, take a picture with me while I have my phone out." I made sure to take the picture with the men in the background so we would have their faces in case we needed to find out who they were.

"What time is the limousine picking us up tonight?" I asked. I looked at my watch as if to check whether we had enough time to do everything.

"Eight is when we start signing autographs, so I think the limo is picking us up at seven o'clock," Kea replied. "Are we wearing our usual outfits we wear when we perform?"

I said, "I think that's a good idea. Well, we had better go and start getting ready. We don't want to disappoint our fans." We got our things and left, knowing that inquiring minds wanted to know and that eyes were following us as we walked down the beach. The men could have been trying to find out what we knew about the murder, or they could have just been nosy. We had fed them some information they would probably talk about for a long time. I still couldn't go by the scene of the crime, so we went the long way home. We made sure none of the guys followed us back to our apartment.

"I want crab legs tonight, so let's go to the seafood restaurant up the street. We can walk there," Lucy said.

"That's a great idea," Kea said.

I said, "I want to take a shower as quick as possible to get the creepy man cooties off of me, and I am sticky and sandy from the beach."

We got ready pretty quickly. We walked up the street and went into The Lucky Crab restaurant. It had all kinds of metal ocean decor on the walls. It was painted coral blue with white accents. The booths were also coral and had very high sides. I liked it because it would give us some privacy just in case we had some business to discuss.

We all ordered crab legs. We were all hungry, so conversation was limited to "Yummy" and "This is delicious." There was a seafood market adjoining the restaurant. "I just love the smell of fresh seafood," Lucy said.

As we were eating dinner, Kea said, "Something just came to me. I smelled gas at the sand dune when we discovered the hand in the sand. I thought the smell was from David since he had just come from the oil company. Art also smelled like gas in that blue van." We all looked at each other.

"It has to be connected to the Seaside Oil Company!" I exclaimed. "I don't suppose that David did this terrible thing."

"That would be very disappointing to me, because I could have sworn that David was an honest, sincere young man," Roberta said.

We finished eating and walked by the gas station. We needed to walk after all the crab legs we had consumed. A big oil truck was sitting there with two tanks on the back, but there was no one around. It was late, and the gas station was closed. I wondered why the truck would be there in the middle of the night unless David owned it. I had an idea. It was time for some sleuthing.

I explained my idea as we walked back to the apartment. "Moonshiners would hire oil companies to deliver their moonshine. They would have two tanks on the large tanker trucks. One would have oil in it, and the other would have moonshine in it. If the federal agents stopped the oil truck drivers, they would show them the tank with the oil in it. I saw that the large oil truck at the gas station had two tanks on the back. We have to go back up there and see what's in those tanks. I hope everyone has some dark clothes so we won't be seen. Kea, you don't have to go up there if you are afraid, but if there's any way you can, it would be appreciated."

Kea asked, "Why?"

I said, "We might need your nose to smell if oil or gas was in the tank if it is empty. Roberta, can you be our lookout?"

I got my backpack of supplies including a knife, gloves, and a towel. I took out some things such as a cookbook and my allergy medicines. Lucy said, "Why do you have those things?"

I said, "I have no idea. I take these things to the music venue when I cater. I should have emptied it before I left home." We all dressed in black and walked over to the gas station with our flashlights. It was very dark, and we tried not to use our flashlights so no one would see us. There was one single light blinking inside the service station, which gave out an eerie aura.

Kea climbed the ladder, opened up the lid, and looked in the first tank using her flashlight. She climbed down and said, "It is empty and smells like gas."

We anxiously waited for her to look in the other tank to see whether it told a different story. She started climbing up when we heard Roberta stirring.

"Quick! Climb down, Kea. There is a car slowing down. We need to hide!" Roberta said excitedly. We ran and hid behind the building and waited.

"Okay, the coast is clear," Roberta whispered.

Kea started climbing up the ladder to the other tank, but she nearly fell off when a seagull flew over, screeching. She slowly opened up the tank. She started whisper screaming. "Oh no! Oh no! It's a—"

I quickly said, "Shh! Wait until you get down before you tell us!"

Kea sailed down the ladder and said, "I saw an arm and a leg and a head and other body parts! That tank had a dead body in it! My nose started burning, and I smelled acid."

I said, "So whoever had done this hoped to dispose of the body. What do we do now? Do we call the police?"

I pulled out the knife from my backpack. I was afraid the truck would be gone before the police investigated. I slashed the tires. The truck wouldn't get too far now if anybody tried to move it. As soon as I had done this, we ran back to the apartment. As we were running, I tried to call Zach, but he didn't answer, so I called the police department. I knew I would get another butt chewing, but the police needed to know about this.

We went back to the apartment and had some moonshine. We saw blue lights flashing from our apartment. The police must have called Zach, because he called shortly after I had called 9-1-1. I told him what we had done. He said, "I will be by to see you in the morning after I check this out tonight. Do not go anywhere or snoop anymore!"

Chapter 7

After we ate breakfast, we all twiddled our thumbs. We all brought a little food and supplies from home. We were going to have to go back to the store soon. I lost my pleasing personality when I didn't eat, so I somehow managed to load up on lots of fluffy pancakes. There was a knock at the door. It was Zach. He said, "I am here bright and early this morning."

I said, "I am not so bright this early in the morning."

Zach said, "What possessed you to look in the oil truck tanks?"

I explained, "My daddy owned an oil company, and he told me that a long time ago, moonshiners would hire oil companies with trucks that had two tanks on them to deliver their product, so I had the idea that maybe both tanks didn't have oil or gas in them. It seemed strange for it to be there at night."

"Have you found out anything?" Roberta asked. Zach said nothing.

"Do you know if it was acid in that truck?" Kea said. "I smelled something that really burned my nose when I looked in that tank." Mum was still the word.

"Do you think you have enough to identify the person now that you've found what could possibly be the rest of the body or was it a totally different person?" Lucy asked.

He went on ignoring the questions. Then: "Since this is going to be in the newspaper tomorrow, I can tell you what I know. We are trying to find out if there are any missing persons, so we are giving more information out than usual. Yes, the body parts were in acid, and it was a woman with a missing hand."

We all looked at Kea approvingly, because she had smelled acid around the oil truck.

Zach continued, "Hopefully the coroner can identify the woman from what was left if she is not a tourist. It will take weeks if not months to ID her if that woman isn't local. There is only one person missing in the area. A woman named Harriet Shelton was reported missing by her family."

Lucy said, "Can't you arrest David? The truck was at his place of business."

Zach said, "He is certainly a suspect, but we have no proof that he did it, because that is not his truck. Let us do our job. You hear me?" He opened the door and stomped out of the room, then turned around and said, "That was a great idea to slash the tires to keep the truck in place until we could get there!" He smiled and walked out the door.

As soon as he left, Lucy got out her laptop and started doing her computer magic. She investigated who Harriet Shelton was. Soon she said, "Harriet Shelton is a bookkeeper for a large company called Seaside Corporation in the next town. Here are her social media addresses. Some of you, look up this info while I do more background checks."

Jackie looked her up and said, "Harriet seems to be a nice woman from what I'm seeing on social media. It shows pictures of her with her family. It also shows her participating in numerous community events and donating to different organizations. The comments made under her pictures by other people are all positive. No one seems to troll her or be mean about her."

After a while, Lucy said, "She has no criminal record and is married with two young children. The company she works for, Seaside Corporation, owns half of everything around us. They are huge."

I said, "We need to find out who the owner or owners are and what they are up to. We need to keep an eye on David at the Seaside Oil Company and find Art with the blue van."

The next day we decided to go back to town and have lunch. I was eager to try some more local seafood. It was a highly walkable town, with an easy pace of life that was heavenly for those who didn't want the hustle and bustle of busier beach towns. There was a gorgeous view of the sound with marshlands and fishing boats going by as we grabbed a leisurely lunch. Then we went to the local grocery store and bought some more food to cook at the apartment. A man was putting groceries on the shelf.

I went up to him and asked, "Do you know anyone in this town by the name of Art?" Then my nose grew like Pinocchio as I lied and told him, "There was a note on the door of the apartment that we are renting addressed to someone named Art. We didn't know if it could have been a tourist or someone local."

The guy replied, "I know just about everyone in this town, and I don't know an Art."

I thanked him, and we left. We asked a couple of more people the same question, and no one had heard of him. I wondered if he had made up a fictitious name. We could basically keep an eye on David from our apartment windows. We were afraid to go to the service station and be too nosy since he could possibly be the murderer.

Chapter 8

The Salteens waited patiently for two days before I called Zach at the police station. I said, "Have you found out anything yet?"

He said, "State forensics checked DNA and dental records from the body, and we have identified the woman in the oil truck as Harriet Shelton. The family identified the gold ring she had on her hand, and they described the clothes she had on the day she went missing, and they were the same ones in the tank of the oil truck. The material hadn't disintegrated in the acid. Harriet hadn't been dead that long, so the acid hadn't had time to work, and the head did look like her. I grew up with her. She was my neighbor."

We looked up Harriet's obituary and decided that we needed to go to her funeral. But none of us had funeral clothes, so we had to go shopping. We all bought a little black dress at one of the local boutiques. We decided to go to the funeral home the night before the funeral, when the family was having visitation, in hopes that we could talk to someone.

We were able to walk from our apartment. We were trying to figure out what to do or say on the way, but we had no plan when we walked into the building with all those strangers. The parking lot was full, and there were people inside and flowing out of the building. I guess everyone was as curious as we were. Also, everyone in town probably knew her.

The funeral home was immaculate inside and out. I didn't see a speck of dust inside or a weed outside. It was well lit on the outside and plainly visible without being garish.

As we walked in, I saw Kea wiggle her nose, because there are always scents of fresh flowers in every funeral home. There was muted indirect lighting from lamps. It wasn't a place for fluorescent or neon lights. We walked down the hall, which was full of people, still not knowing what to say or do. Some of them nodded at us and said hello. We walked into a room with comfortable-looking, well-upholstered, clean, modest, and middle-of-the-road-style furniture.

A man came over to us. I guess he recognized the lost looks on our faces. He said, "Hi, I'm the funeral director, Ralph Moran. I want to welcome you."

I said, "Hello, I'm Shirley Ann Dalton. Your building is beautiful. You really keep it in good shape. My cousin's husband back home is the director of our funeral home." He was very cordial, and we immediately had a bond. He asked where we were from.

Then Jackie whispered in my ear, "The mayor is in the next room, canvassing."

I said to Ralph, "Excuse me."

A woman was standing in the corner, crying. She walked up to us. "Hi, I'm Sandra. How did you know my sister?"

I said, "We didn't know her. I was the one who found her hand, and we were so devastated over the situation that we came to pay our respects to the family."

Sandra hesitated and said, "That's nice."

She started to walk off, but Roberta chimed in, "Do you have any idea why this happened and who could have done such a terrible thing?"

"No," Sandra said and began sobbing again.

Lucy said, "Was anything going on at work that you know of?"

"No," Sandra said.

I said, "I know we sound like busybodies, but her death has also traumatized us. Harriet wasn't involved in drugs or anything like that?"

"No," Sandra shouted. "She was a wonderful, law-abiding citizen who wouldn't hurt a fly. Go away!"

The mayor came over and put his arm around her. He looked at us, nodded, and in a soft, sweet voice said, "Sandra, is everything okay?"

"No," she said. "These ladies are asking questions about Harriet."

The mayor gave us the stink eye as he hugged her, so we knew it was time to leave.

"Well, that went well," Jackie said as we walked back to the apartment. "The mayor did seem to have genuine concern and cared about Sandra."

The next day we decided that we shouldn't go to the church for the funeral since we were probably persona non grata. We decided the best thing to do would be to sit outside and see who came to the funeral. We were going to look for Art of the blue van and any other suspicious-looking individuals.

We went to the funeral early the next day so we could have a good view of everyone who came. The only thing of interest was when a big limousine pulled up and a distinguished-looking man got out. Lucy said, "I wonder if that is Harriet's rich boss, the owner of the Seaside Corporation." He seemed rather stoic, unemotional, and aloof. He shook hands with several people as he went in.

Roberta said, "Isn't that the kid who was in the Seaside Shop? I think his name is Oliver."

"Yes, I think you're right," Lucy said.

Kea said, "There's the mayor walking in with the family. I wonder if he is related to Harriet or if he thought he was in good enough standing to walk in with them so he could get reelected." Once the people had gone into the church, there wasn't much for us to watch for. We wanted to stay and see what happened when the people came out of the church after the services. We all packed into one car, and it was hot.

"Get your sharp tailbone off of me," Kea said to me. We were getting impatient. I sat there and tried to think of something to get our minds off the situation.

"What is your favorite drunken memory?" I asked.

Jackie said, "I got drunk and lost my bathing suit in the ocean once."

I told them the funniest drunk story I had ever heard. "This guy I know was telling me about how he and his wife got drunk one night. They had gone on a trip and were on the way home. They got frisky and got naked in the car. The guy put his clothes back on. His wife had passed out. When they got back to their hometown, he pulled into the local drive-through, which was closed. He nudged his wife and said, 'What would you like to eat, honey?' She woke up, scrambling to try to cover herself. Then she realized the place was closed, and he almost got killed."

We all had a good laugh. My next question was, "What is your favorite gift? My favorite gift was when my husband and I were dating. He didn't have any money, and he stopped on the side of the road and gave me flowers that were growing there."

We all jumped when someone knocked on my car window. It was Zach. I put my window down.

"Hello, ladies," he said. "Do you know of any reason why you should be here?"

"No!" we said in unison.

Zach said, "Well, then, I think it is time for you to go." So we left.

Chapter 9

We are all sitting on our apartment balcony, trying to think of a new strategy to find the murderer. Nothing eventful had happened at the funeral, so we were all disappointed. We might have found something out if we could have stayed longer. Harriet was going to be buried in the church cemetery.

The breeze from the ocean was comforting. "When I was doing research for the moonshine festival play," I said, "I remembered one moonshiner's daughter telling me that she had to stay home with her baby sister while the rest of the family went to the big city to sell their moonshine. They left one jug of 'shine' at home. She saw a line of black cars coming down the driveway as she was changing the baby's diaper. She knew it had to be government agents. Back then, they had only cloth diapers. She put the jug of moonshine in the dirty diaper pail. It was where they put dirty diapers in a solution until they washed them. The agents searched everywhere for some moonshine. They would never think to look in a dirty diaper pail. After they left, the lady said she took the jug of moonshine to the creek and washed it off and put it back on the shelf.

"I think maybe David did this since everything points to him right now. The oil truck was at his place of business, and the hand was near where he works. We need to find the murder weapon. He could have it at the gas station. That might seal the deal on who did this terrible act. Where do you think he could have hidden it so no one would think to look?"

There were many guesses. Kea said, "Behind the toilet."

Lucy said, "In the toolbox."

Roberta said, "Inside a vending machine."

Jackie said, "In the trash can between the can and the bag."

I said, "Maybe he threw it in the ocean."

None of these ideas seemed likely. We decided we would go and take a look at the service station tonight.

The service station was a rather small structure located right across the street from our apartment building. There was a vacant lot on either side of the building. It was basically in a residential area with some nearby apartments and houses rented to tourists. There weren't many places rented in this area right now, and there was very little traffic this late at night. It was as hot as blue blazes, and my nervousness made it seem even warmer. Roberta whispered as we got closer, "I'll be the lookout again."

Jackie said, "Whistle real loud if someone comes."

We crossed the street and went into the vacant lot beside the building so the lights at the front of the station wouldn't reveal us. We slowly went around to the back of the building. Kea's voice trembled. "I'm scared."

Roberta said, "You help me be the lookout. You get on one side of the building, and I'll get on the other side."

Some windows were open at the back of the Seaside Oil Company. David probably did that at night to keep the grease and gas odors from permeating the whole inside. The windows were low enough to be manageable.

I opened my backpack, handed everyone gloves, and said, "Put these on so your fingerprints won't be on anything." I pushed out the window screens.

Lucy whispered, "You weigh less than anyone else, so we'll form a human pyramid for you to climb on."

I climbed in through the window and fell on the floor, landing on my rear end. "Ouch," I whispered loudly.

The others were mumbling, "Are you okay?"

"I'm fine. I have a sore derriere though," I said. I used my flashlight to find my way around and found a side door to let everyone else in. I put the screen back on the window.

This door was connected to the garage part of the station. One area had snack machines and a desk with a cash register. It also had a few chairs where people could sit and wait for their car engines to be fixed. There was a door at the back leading to a bathroom. Attached to this waiting area was a two-bay garage with large lift-up doors to allow the cars to drive in. One bay had a lift, in which the cars were driven. They were lifted by an electric motor, and then the mechanics could walk under the cars and work on various parts.

The other bay had a grease pit. The car was driven over the pit, which was a large concrete rectangle. It was a little smaller than a vehicle but deep enough to be the height of an average man. Steps led down to the pit, where the mechanics could work on the car overhead. They kept metal buckets down there to collect grease and oil.

I whispered, "Lucy, you check out things in the garage area with me. Jackie, you look in the desk area and bathroom. There are front windows, so be careful with the flashlight."

Jackie said, "I think I'll be able to see enough from the lights in front so I won't have to use the flashlight. Let's make it fast."

We looked everywhere including file cabinets, desk drawers, and the counters behind things. We didn't find anything that looked like it could be a murder weapon. It was so hard to keep quiet and not shine lights where they could be seen from the road.

Then an idea came to my mind. The murder weapon was in the grease pit!

I was very familiar with grease pits since my daddy had owned a service station and oil company when I was growing up. I said, "Okay, we can't seem to find anything, so what about the grease pit?"

I shined the flashlight down into the pit. We all looked down into the big hole, and it was a "holey" mess.

Everyone looked at me and one by one said, "I'm not getting into that thing."

"I guess it's up to little ole me," I said. I got a towel out of my backpack and we laid it down. We also found some paper towels to catch the mess when I got out of the hole. We made a paper towel carpet to the door so hopefully there would be no grease anywhere. I was going to ruin my shoes, but I left them on, because I was afraid I would cut my feet on the mess at the bottom. It had several inches of oil and grease. Two large metal buckets would normally collect the grease and oil, but they were overturned. That was very odd to me since most of the time the metal buckets were emptied daily into a collection barrel.

I held my breath and dove in. It smelled terrible in that hole. I was glad Kea didn't have to do this, because the odor may have blown her nose off. This was truly the most disgusting thing ever. "Oh, my goodness. This is so gross," I whispered. I trudged through inch by inch. I was beginning to think this was a lost cause when I hit something. "I feel something!"

"What is it?" Lucy asked.

"I don't know. I'm trying to figure out how I can get it out of there without having to do a nosedive." I was so glad I had gloves on. I picked up what I thought was a handle and gave it to my friends.

"It is a huge knife!" Jackie said. "Don't wipe it off! Lay it on some paper towels." Lucy and Jackie picked up the paper towels after me. We figured out how to lock the door from the inside, closed it, and ran back to the apartment. I took my shoes off, threw them in the outside trash can, and entered our place.

I said, "Now I know why the murderer didn't clean up the grease pit. Those metal buckets were deliberately toppled over so he or she could hide the murder weapon. The knife was too long to hide in the bucket." The Salteens all agreed with me. At least, that was what we all thought.

Roberta said, "The only thing I hate about this is that if this is the murder weapon, then it might be enough to convict David, and I don't want it to be him." We all agreed.

Kea asked me, "How is your derriere?"

I replied, "I think I need some ice." Now we had the dreaded call the next day to the police station to speak to my new best friend. Then we had some moonshine.

I called Zach the next morning and told him he needed to come right over immediately, because I had something he needed. I didn't want to get grease and oil in one of our cars if we took it to the police station. He could get it in the police car.

Zach arrived. "What have you girls been up to this time?"

"We think we have something you need," Jackie said.

Zach said, "What is that?"

Jackie handed him the knife wrapped in the paper towel and said, "A knife we think is the murder weapon. We found it last night when we went to the Seaside Oil Company behind here."

I was sitting on ice, trying to soothe my sore, black-and-blue buttocks. The Salteens turned their heads and looked at me. "I had an idea that the murder weapon might be in an obvious place," I said, "and since the body was at the service station, I thought the weapon might be there also."

Zach said, "Where on earth was this messy thing?"

Roberta said, "It was in the grease pit."

Zach said, "How did you figure that out?" The Salteens all turned their heads and looked at me.

I said, "We looked everywhere else, and that was a place most people would think was too disgusting to look, so I went for it." I gave him all the rest of the details.

Zach said, "Why do you keep wincing, and why are you sitting on a bag of ice?"

I said, "I left that part out. I fell climbing into the open window and bruised my rear end." I think he was trying to keep a straight face.

"You do know that breaking and entering is a crime," Zach said in a stern voice.

Kea said, "We didn't break a thing."

Zach rolled his eyes, carefully took the weapon, and left.

Chapter 10

After Zach left, we fixed breakfast. It was a yummy omelet and some of my sourdough bread. While we were sitting at the table, Lucy said, "I need to dig deeper into the Seaside Corporation. I may need to do a little hacking."

She went into her room to do some quiet research, and rest of us lay around like beached whales. I was like a beached whale with a sore tail.

Later, she said, "I found out that Seaside Corporation owns a lot of gas stations and markets that sell gas. The corporation also owns the Seaside Shop. I wonder if it is connected at all to the one David owns." Lucy couldn't seem to find anything else, so we decided that maybe we should pay a visit to the Seaside Corporation.

We went to the place listed as the address for the business, and it was a very unappealing building with an old shack in the back. It looked like a rustic beach cottage that had been turned into an office. A sign out front told us we were at the right place. We had felt like it was going to be some skyscraper with mirrored sides since the owner or owners seemed to have a lot of property. One car was parked out front.

We still had no idea why we were going in there and what we were going to say. We were going to wing it. The man we had seen in the limousine at the funeral stepped out of his office. "Hi, my name is Matthew Hutzler. Can I help you?"

"Yes, my name is Shirley Ann," I said, "and these are all of my friends. I was the one who found the hand in the sand at the beach. We were so upset that we just wanted to come and see where the dear woman who died worked."

"She will really be missed. She was an asset to this place. I don't know how I will ever replace her."

"Do you know of any reason she was killed? Was she into anything that could have made this happen?" I wanted to ask him the drug question, since people at the bar had hinted that it could be a cause for the murder, but that question hadn't gone too well the last time I asked it at the funeral home.

"No. She was kind to everyone, and everyone loved her. Her family was great. I don't know of any problems going on. As far as I know, she had never even drunk a drop of alcohol her whole life, much less done any drugs."

Eureka! That answered my question.

We started to leave, and I leaned against the doorsill. "We are all sorry for your loss. We just have had a hard time getting over the discovery and just needed to come by."

"I know I didn't answer any questions you might have. You might want to quit asking because it could get you in trouble. Somebody around here is dangerous."

"Yes sir."

We left immediately. That was twice we had been warned except for the forty-nine hundred times Zach had warned us. Maybe somebody at the Seaside Corporation had murdered poor Harriet. A lot of crimes were committed because of power and money.

When we got back in the car and drove away, we had to catch our breaths after the latest threat. I said, "While I was leaning against the doorsill and we were being threatened, I stole some keys so we can get back in there later on tonight." I got a lot of looks from my comrades, and they weren't sweet, adorable looks.

Some famous race car drivers came from running moonshine. They had to be able to drive fast to get away from the law. We decided to rent a car with a fast engine for this next venture so no one would recognize our cars since everyone seemed to know our business.

Jackie was our designated driver. She had a little sports car and loved to drive fast. We may need to make a fast escape.

We all had a different assignment for breaking into the Seaside Corporation. Lucy was going to copy computer data. I was going to look in the file cabinets. Roberta was going to look in desk drawers. Jackie was going to stay in the getaway car, and Kea was going to be the lookout and warn us if anyone was coming.

We went to the Seaside Corporation again that night. We parked at the back of the building. We easily got in using the keys.

"Let's quickly do our assignments and get out of here," Lucy said.

We were all frantically searching when the phone suddenly rang, and we nearly jumped out of our skin. I took a picture of a list of employees, which I thought might be helpful. Roberta found only obvious things someone would find in a desk drawer like scissors, paper clips, and pens. There were beautiful pictures of Harriet's family still sitting on what we assumed was her desk. One of us took a picture of that.

Harriet had a beautiful little girl with long blonde hair and blue eyes, and she had a son who was just as adorable. Those children would never know their mother. We had to find the killer.

Suddenly, we heard someone walking on the gravel outside and quickly ducked. We waited and then realized it was Kea.

None of us found anything we thought we could use. I guessed we would have to wait and see whether Lucy could find out anything from what she had downloaded to her drive from their computer system. As soon as she was finished, I quickly put the keys back in their place on the nail near the doorsill.

We pulled out of the parking lot of the Seaside Corporation. As we were driving down the road, we all thought we saw the mayor in his fancy car. We turned around, and he was turning into the Seaside Corporation. It would have been too obvious for us to go back and see what was going on.

"Boy, that was close," Kea said. "He almost caught us there."

"I know. I wonder why he was going to the Seaside Corporation," Roberta said.

"Maybe he was just turning around," Lucy said.

After we got back to the apartment, we looked at the list of employees. We didn't find Art's name on there. Lucy didn't find Art's name on anything she had researched either, but she found out the names of the men at the Seaside Shop, which was also owned by the Seaside Corporation. John Davis and Oliver Garrison were two names we needed to remember, though they might just be two pot-smoking kids who had a temporary summer job there.

I said, "I'm beginning to get overload now. I need a vision board to write all of this down. My head is spinning."

Chapter 11

The next morning while we were eating breakfast, Lucy came running into the living room after doing research in her bedroom. "I found the names of the oil truck drivers! One of them is William Shelton, and the other one is Oliver Garrison. I wonder if they are related to Harriett. Shelton is her married name, and Garrison is her maiden name. Oliver Garrison is also one of the employees at the Seaside Shop." So now we knew the oil truck belonged to the Seaside Corporation. They had sold the service station to David, but they must still provide him gas for his business. Seaside Corporation had to be involved in all this!

"This area is small enough that this probably isn't a coincidence," I said. "I'm sure a lot of people have kin folks working with them, especially if Seaside Corporation is one of the largest employers in the area. We need to find out William and Oliver's addresses and follow them."

"Oh no, here we go again!" Kea said. "You're going to get us killed! I want to see my grandbabies again. We have to stop this!" Kea loved her grandchildren more than life itself. She helped her daughter while she worked by carpooling them to all their extracurricular activities and kept them a lot during the summers when they weren't in school. I'm sure this situation was hard on her daughter and that the kids missed their grandmother.

"Kea, if you are scared, then take your car and go home. I have to figure this out," I said. "I can't imagine living life so carefully that there are no signs that I have lived at all."

Kea said, "I can't leave y'all down here! I also want to know what happened, but I just want us to be careful."

"I get it. I'm scared too, but I can't just sit here. We have to be proactive. So far, we have found out more than the police have."

Kea took a deep breath and said, "Let's go then."

We all took a nighttime walk on the beach. There was no one out there but us. Being here was like having our own private beach. The cool sand felt good on my feet. If you aren't barefoot, you're overdressed at the beach. The moon shone a bright light on the ocean as the waves occasionally washed the sand off our feet.

Kea said, "Walking on the beach is like a sedative."

"I agree," Roberta said. "I bet my mama is looking down on us now, protecting us."

"I miss home. I hope we can resolve this quickly," I said. Then we walked back to our temporary home.

Lucy found the addresses of the two oil truck drivers. We figured they were working during the day, so our best chance of looking them up would be at night. The term *moonshine* was coined from the fact that the work had to be done at night by the light of the moon so no one would catch them. I was beginning to think we were sort of like moonshiners since most of our work was at night. It was time for our nightly sip before we went to bed.

Chapter 12

We went to the beach the next morning. It was nice just to sit there with the waves hitting our feet and not thinking about what had gone on over the last few days … maybe. David came down to see us. "How are you all doing? Have you heard anything?"

We all looked at each other. I didn't know what to say, because we might have sealed his fate if that knife we had found was the murder weapon. I said, "No. Have you?"

He said, "The police came again and asked me all sorts of questions about the oil truck. I don't know anything about that. It doesn't belong to me. Sometimes Billy, the driver, will leave it there overnight if I am the last place he delivers gas to, and he can walk home from there. He lives right down the street."

Lucy kicked her feet in the water. "Is he the only driver?"

Oh boy. Maybe we can find out some good info right here, I thought.

"No, the other driver is Oliver Garrison. Billy works full-time, and Oliver works part-time. He is the brother of Harriet, the lady who was murdered."

"As small as this place is, I guess everybody knows everybody," Jackie said as she rubbed suntan lotion on her arms.

"Yes. That's right. Ollie has had a lot on him here lately. He's been working really hard with two jobs. He carries oil and works at the Seaside Shop in town. He didn't need the death of Harriet on top of it all."

"What happened?" I curiously asked.

David hesitated and said, "I really don't want to talk about him in a bad way. He's healthy and doing well now."

After we got back to the apartment, we tried to figure out what David had meant. I said, "He talked about Oliver being healthy now, which means he suffered from an illness of some sort. It could be legal or illegal such as drugs."

Lucy said, "He would have told us if it was legal like cancer or something. It has to be drugs. I'm just glad that he's doing well now, according to David."

Kea said, "I do remember thinking I smelled something besides weed in that little shop that day. It was gas. I guess that is because Oliver drives the oil truck. I guess the guy David called 'Billy' is a nickname for the driver Lucy said was William Shelton."

I said, "Let's do some surveillance on Harriet's brother tonight."

Lucy said, "I'll find out his address. Dress cool for tonight in case we have to sit in the car for a while."

Kea said, "I'll drive my car."

I said, "Do you know how to follow a car without getting caught?"

"I've seen them do it on television." She got some laughs and looks of disbelief from us.

Later that night, Kea drove past Oliver's house. "He must be home since there is a car in the driveway and a light on. I am going to park across the street and down two or three houses in hopes that no one will notice."

We sat there for quite a while. Doing surveillance wasn't for us. It was hard for us to keep quiet for long. Suddenly, we saw activity; Oliver was leaving the house. Kea followed him as best she could.

Jackie said, "Don't follow too closely. He might see us. There isn't that much traffic in this little town."

Kea said, "Jackie, we've gotten in trouble with half the town by now, so we may as well add him to the list."

Lucy said, "We're going in the direction of the Seaside Corporation. He's turning into Seaside. What is he doing here at night when it is closed?"

"Oh my gosh. There are several cars parked in the back at the shack," Kea said as she slowly went past the business. "What do you think is going on back there? Is it a party place or for meetings?" She turned around, and by the time we went by the place again, Oliver was leaving.

"That was fast," Roberta said.

We followed him for several miles. We were still thinking about what was going on in the shack behind Seaside Corporation.

"Isn't this the same road of the church where Harriet's funeral was held?" Lucy asked.

About that time, Oliver gave a turn signal. He was going to the graveyard behind the church. None of us felt good about this. Kea went down the road a bit and parked the car. We walked and could see where Oliver had parked in the cemetery.

I whispered, "Why would he be going to a cemetery at night? I know moonshiners used to hide their stills at family cemeteries because no one would think to look there, but I don't think he would be hiding anything at a public cemetery."

Lucy put her hand to her lips to make me be quiet. We crept along and hid behind trees and tombstones. We could hear something as we got closer. It was Oliver sobbing at his sister's grave. Then his words: "I didn't mean for this to happen to you. I will find out who's behind this."

Oliver left after a few minutes, and we stayed in our positions until we thought it was safe to go to the car.

When we finally got in the car, Jackie said, "What was he talking about?"

I said, "I don't know, but I'm more curious than ever now. I just want to know how we can find out what is going on."

Chapter 13

The next day I went to get some supplies at the local grocery store. The people there were talking to each other about the arrest that had been made. I tried to listen behind the shelf of canned tomatoes but couldn't find out any details. I thought I might have to call Zach again, but I spotted a newspaper with the headline that said, ARREST MADE IN LOCAL MURDER. I bought it so maybe we could find out some information without having to call the police; then maybe we could go home.

I couldn't wait until I got back to the apartment. I read the newspaper article in the car in the grocery parking lot. They had arrested David! I wondered if Oliver knew about it. I rushed to the apartment to tell everyone the news.

Kea read the newspaper and said, "We have solved the murder. Now we can go home."

I said, "I guess so. I just hate that we had the wrong impression of David."

We all went to our rooms and were starting to pack to go home when I got a phone call from an unknown number. It was David calling from jail. I put him on speaker so all the Salteens could hear what he had to say.

He said, "I know you all have been trying to find Harriet's killer. The police have got the wrong guy. I did not kill Harriet. We dated in high school. I loved her at one time. You have got to help the police find the real killer."

I said, "I don't know what else we can do, David."

He said, "Please help me. I swear I didn't do it."

I said, "I'll talk to my friends and see what they say. We can't stay away from home much longer." We hung up. I looked at the Salteens and asked, "What do you want to do?"

"Call Zach and see what he says. If he has doubts, we have to stay. If he has proof, then we can go home," Lucy said.

I called Zach. I asked, "I heard that the police arrested David. Do you believe he did this? Do you have any doubts?"

There was a moment of hesitation. I guess he was about to explode. He exclaimed, "Are you kidding me? Why are you still asking these questions? You are not a police officer!"

I asked again, "Are you sure and have no doubts and have solid proof that David is the one who murdered Harriet? David called me and swore he didn't do it."

"No, we do not have proof that he did it, but all signs lead to it, and I feel like we will have proof soon."

I asked him whether David's fingerprints had been found on the knife or oil truck, and he said no.

I disconnected the phone and looked at my friends. I said, "I need a roll call of who wants to stay and who wants to go."

Lucy said, "Stay."

Roberta said, "Stay."

Jackie said, "Stay."

Kea said, "Let's unpack. We're staying." The Salteens decided to stay and find out for sure who had killed Harriet. We all felt that maybe the police had arrested the wrong guy.

Roberta said, "We all had strong intuition from the beginning that David didn't do it."

I said, "I agree. I know at first, I thought he did it, but now it just doesn't seem right to me. Why would he call complete strangers to help him get his name cleared? He said he spent all of his money buying the business, so I'm sure he doesn't have the money for a private investigator. That's one reason why he was living with his mom. It just seems odd to me that all of it is at his place of business. Anybody with any sense would take the body somewhere else. A normal crook would get rid of any evidence. It almost seems like he is being set up to take the blame."

We talked about Otis's suggestion that the spouse be looked at first. I wanted to see Harriet's husband. Lucy looked up his address, and we were on our way to Pleasant Drive. It was a Saturday, so we were hoping that everyone was home from work and school. We saw lots of kids playing in the streets under the palmetto fronds. I knew we were at the right house when I saw Harriet's adorable little girl playing in the yard. I recognized her from the picture on Harriet's desk.

We rang the doorbell. A man came to the door. I said, "Hi, my name is Shirley Ann Dalton. I am the one who discovered Harriet's hand in the sand dune."

He looked puzzled. "Hello, I am James, Harriet's husband."

"My friends and I couldn't leave until the murderer was found. We are packing to go home since they found who killed Harriet. Before we leave, we wanted you to know how sorry we are that this happened to your family."

James hesitated and then said, "I can't believe it was David. He has always been kind to us. He had no reason that I know of to do that."

Roberta said, "Do you know anyone who would have a reason?"

James answered, "Harriet was very nervous and anxious several days before this happened. I asked her several times if she was okay. She only said that work was getting to her. She had always liked her job and her boss, so I don't know if she was really busy or if she had found something out that she didn't need to know."

"What was her job there?" Lucy said.

He replied, "She did everything. She answered the phones and was the bookkeeper."

Kea asked, "Were there any questionable employees there?"

James said, "I knew everyone there, but you never know about people. Harriet was alone most of the time except when her boss came in or when someone came to the office to pay a bill. Ollie, Harriet's brother, had struggled with drugs, but he went to rehab. He has two jobs and is doing great. Billy also carries oil on the tanker for the company. He grew up here, and I've never heard anybody say anything negative about him. I don't know much about the guy Ollie works with at the Seaside Shop. He's not from around here. He moved here a year or two ago with his brother from Texas."

We heard, "Daddy!"

He said, "I need to go to make sure my children are safe and behaving."

We left. This situation was getting even more mysterious. Kea said, "If her husband is guilty, he would not be saying those things about David. He would want to point the finger at him."

The Salteens all agreed.

Chapter 14

"What do you think we need to do now?" I asked.

Jackie said, "We need to talk to Oliver. We have to figure out how to do that since he is so busy."

Roberta said, "I think we need to investigate the other truck driver, Billy, and the guy who worked with Oliver at the Seaside Shop, John Davis."

We decided to organize our plans for the rest of the day. We went to lunch at the Seaside Café and strategized.

Kea said, "We need to do one of these tasks with all of us together. I don't want our group to split up. It could be dangerous. I don't do danger."

"Shirley Ann swam in danger in that grease pit. We are still swimming in danger," Lucy said.

Jackie said, "Let's wait outside the Seaside Shop until Oliver gets off work and talk to him. Let's ride by the shop after we finish eating and see if he is there."

We rode by the Seaside Shop and knew he was working there. Lucy said, "That's his car. I remember it from following him to the cemetery." We parked out back across the street. We waited for three hours in the heat, with most of us sunburned. We would have to sneak out of the car one at a time to go to the bathroom. That was miserable. He finally came out the back door to where his car was parked.

We immediately got out of the car and walked over to him. He seemed startled, and when he realized who we were, he didn't seem too excited. "What can I help you with?" he said.

I wasn't in the mood to beat around the bush. "Do you really think David killed Harriet?"

He said, "That's who the police arrested. They must think he did it. It doesn't really matter what I think."

"But it does. You don't want the wrong person going to jail," Jackie said.

He was beginning to get nervous and kept glancing back at the shop. "Look, I don't know who did it, and I need to go to work at my other job. Please leave me alone. This could be dangerous for you and especially for me." He got into his car and left us standing there.

Chapter 15

We got back in our car. Lucy said, "He must have gotten tangled up with the wrong people doing drugs. I may be wrong, but there's something fishy going on. Why did he keep looking back at the shop?"

Roberta said, "The next person who needs our attention is John Davis, the other guy in the Seaside Shop. It was almost like Oliver was scared he would see us talking to him. He's not from around here, so I think the only way we're going to find out anything about him is to follow him."

We all agreed.

We left and drove around to look at the pretty little beach town. We all had had too much sun to go back to the beach and sit in the sun, so we decided to sightsee. We drove around and looked at the houses on the ocean and got house envy. Some were polished and sophisticated. Others were casual and rustic. Most of them had broad porches with large rafters and stilts underneath. All of them were unique and charming in a punch bowl of colors.

When it was time for the Seaside Shop to close, we went back and parked where we could see John Davis leave. We followed his car to the grocery store and waited for him to come out of there. He looked our way, and Kea said, "Duck!" We all hit the floor.

He pulled out of the grocery store parking lot, then stopped at several different houses in the area. Kea said, "How are we going to keep him from seeing us?"

I said, "Florence Nightingale once said, 'How very little can be done under the spirit of fear.'" I got an eye roll from my girlfriend.

John always took a small package with him into each house, and we sometimes saw him being handed something back.

We rode by several of the houses where he had stopped and pulled over several houses down from where he was. One lady came out from one of the houses we had pulled in front of and said, "Can I help you?"

I said, "We're lost. Can you tell us the way to 101 Seaside Boulevard?"

She said, "Yes. You take a left at the next stop sign and then go to the end of that road, and you'll be able to see Seaside Boulevard from there. Are you here on vacation?"

I was going to answer when John drove by us in his car. I said, "Bye. We need to go." She looked at me like I had three heads.

John went to what we knew was his address and went inside with a big box from his car's trunk. After that, people started going in and out at his house. No one stayed long.

"John Davis has to be a drug dealer," Jackie said. "Do you think Oliver got messed up with John and that John killed Harriet? We need to find some proof."

We went back to our apartment.

Lucy looked John Davis up on the computer when we got home. She said, "He is from Texas like Harriet's husband said. I looked up his criminal record, and he has been arrested for possession of a controlled substance. I think he has been promoted to a distributor now."

"Why haven't the police discovered all of this when it is obvious to us what is going on? Who could we ask about him who would know?" Roberta asked.

"I'm afraid to ask Zach," I said. "If he knew John Davis was selling drugs, it seems like he would be in jail with David."

Jackie said, "I'm sick of this subject. We're out of moonshine. I researched it, and there is a distillery in a nearby town."

Kea said, "Let's go."

We went to the moonshine distillery that night. They had a restaurant, too, so we had a meal and bought a fresh bottle of peppermint moonshine. It was a huge building with lots of stainless-steel decor. It was sleek and very modern looking. It could probably hold one hundred people whereas the little distillery in our hometown probably couldn't hold any more than twenty, but it was so cozy.

A man came over and spoke to us. "Hi, my name is Hollis, the owner. If y'all need anything, let me know."

Roberta said, "Your moonshine is very smooth."

He said, "I've been busy experimenting with different kinds of booze. I have tried making bourbon and gin moonshine. The Japanese are making something called 'white ale.' I know of some people who are making triple sec and curacao this way and calling it 'moonshine.'"

Jackie said, "The kind of moonshine we are familiar with is unaged whiskey."

We wanted to talk about the next day's activities, but this guy wanted to talk and entertain us. What he had to say was interesting. We also had him take our picture with Otis.

Hollis said, "My grandpa used to make the illegal kind in his barn. Someone kept stealing his 'shine' at night, so he stayed up one night in the barn and hid to see if he could catch who was stealing it. It was a bear! The bear would drink it and stagger away, drunk as it could be. To keep the bear away from his supply, he started leaving the fruit he used to make it with, such as apple peels and cores, on the dirt floor beside the still. The bear would fill up on that and leave his moonshine alone. My grandpa went to prison once for making and selling it, and when he got back, he started making it again. That was the only way people could make a living back then. There weren't many jobs and no factories in the country, so they would use leftover fruit to make moonshine. That same bear came back again to the barn for food!"

"Wow," we all said.

He kept on pontificating. "Today, the term *moonshine* continues to be used to describe illegal product, but now it really means something different. The moonshine anyone purchases at a distillery or liquor store is legal and safe for consumption. Early moonshiners may have distilled illegally, but that doesn't mean they didn't care about what they made. They were proud of what they had made and wanted it to be a quality spirit for their friends, communities, and strangers who bought it."

We said goodbye to Hollis and left the distillery. As we neared the Seaside Oil Company, we noticed that the oil truck was leaving and that Billy was driving it. I said, "That is odd, because I remember David saying that Billy left it there at night when David's place of business was his last stop, and he could walk home from there. I assumed he parked it at David's because there was no room for that big tanker at his house, and it was time for him to get off work. Why would he be leaving in the middle of the night with that big truck? You know he's not delivering oil." The Salteens agreed that it did seem strange.

We arrived at the apartment and were too tired to think. It was time to call it a night. We went to bed with plans about how we would spend our day in the morning.

I went to bed with my head spinning, and it wasn't the moonshine that had done it. Who killed poor Harriet? I knew she was probably an innocent victim in this whole scenario, but I couldn't put the pieces together. Why was Billy driving an oil truck that late at night? Why was John delivering items to people's houses?

I knew two things I was going to do tomorrow. I was going to go to the store, buy some sticky notes, and make a vision board, where we could see what we knew and what we needed to find out. I was also going to buy some ingredients to bake a cake. I was an amateur baker. I loved baking, and it really soothed my soul. I was hoping that something would come to me while I was baking. Besides that, passing out cake to people we might need information from would be a plus. Drunk talk at the bar didn't get people talking, but maybe my cake would.

Chapter 16

Jackie wasn't an early riser, so Roberta, Kea, and I decided to go to the store. Lucy needed to do some more computer sleuthing. "I need to check all of the things that I need to bake a cake with what is in our apartment kitchen," I said. "I know I will need a springform pan and some cake pans, which are not provided in this kitchen. I need new ones anyway, so I will take them back when we go home."

Kea said, "If we ever go home again, I miss my babies. I'll also make a list of some things that we could use. I need some gluten-free items."

Roberta said, "I think we should go to the big-box store in the nearby town since I doubt the local grocer will probably have all of the supplies we need."

We went to the store, and I remembered while I was there that I wanted to purchase some things for a vision board to get ourselves organized. We bought all the cake ingredients and so much more than we would probably ever eat.

I said, "Do you think we have enough?"

Kea said, "We have enough to last at least a year. Let's get some doughnuts on the way home. I saw previously on a sign that they have gluten-free doughnuts."

We brought all the groceries and the warm doughnuts from a little bakery into the apartment. Everyone was awake, so we dug into that box of doughnuts and talked. Jackie said, "One thing that we need to do is to go talk to David in jail to see if he can help us go in a better direction. He has had plenty of time to think about this. We also want him to know that we are trying our best to find out who did this."

Lucy said, "We also need to find out what John Davis is up to. None of us have investigated the other truck driver either. Billy Shelton is a mystery to all of us. His name hasn't come up in any of the conversations until last night when we saw him on that oil truck. I will keep looking on the computer. Social media was what I looked at while you were gone, and they don't seem to be on any of those platforms."

I said, "I nominate Roberta to go talk to David. He can only have one visitor at a time in jail, and your background in psychiatry and your oh-so-clever intuition may come in handy as far as getting something out of him. You're more used to being around those who aren't so stable, so being there may not be as frightening to you. Sometimes I talk before I listen."

Roberta said, "Okay, whose car can I use?"

Kea said, "You can use mine."

Roberta got ready to go to jail to talk to David. I prepared the kitchen for baking the cake, and everyone else went to the beach.

I told them, "Y'all need to get out of my way because the kitchen is very tiny, and I need to think. I had decided to make a toasted coconut cake with a key lime pie layer. This cake was the prize-winning cake in a bake-off contest in my hometown. The cake actually took hours to make. The first thing I did was prepare the piecrust. I had to wait for the cream cheese and butter to soften, so I sat for a while and thought about how much I missed my family. We were going to have to go home soon.

I liked my crust made with vanilla wafers instead of graham crackers. I just liked the flavor better. I had to crush all the wafers and then combine them with the sugar and softened butter. Thank goodness, the little kitchen had a blender. I put the crust in the spring form pan. Most people used this pan only for cheesecake. I had discovered that I couldn't put the pie in a pie pan and expect it to slide onto a cake layer, but it would be easy after I took the sides off the springform pan, and it was also flat. I put the crust in the oven. Then I mixed the key lime pie ingredients. When the oven bell went off, I took the crust out and let it cool. I poured the ingredients on the crust and put it in the refrigerator to harden.

While I worked, I kept thinking about what our next plan of action should be. I thought if we could get a vision board going with what we knew, what we didn't know was what we needed to find out. The board could be a tremendous help. It would at least get us organized.

Next, I started on the cake. I toasted the coconut in the oven. I mixed the cake ingredients, poured them in the new cake pans, and put them in the oven. I thought about my old trusted, rusty cake pans at home. I guess they would be okay with their replacements. Those pans were probably tired from years of use.

Roberta had gotten back to the apartment after visiting David in jail, so we went to the beach to gather up the gang so she would only need to say everything once. I took the cake pans out of the oven to cool, and we talked.

Roberta started to cry. "I just know it's not him. It upset me terribly to see him in that jail."

Lucy said, "You do realize that a murderer can be an excellent con man, and you can't possibly believe everything he says."

Roberta said, "I have worked with psychiatric patients for years. I can read people very well, and my intuition tells me more than ever that David isn't the killer. There are two major things I garnered from that visit. One was that he said Oliver and Billy had both been acting kind of nervous and squirrelly for the past few weeks. They really didn't want to stop and chitchat like they normally did. The other thing is that John Davis had a business on the side in which he made pins and memorabilia for different bands and concerts."

I exclaimed, "So that is what was in those bags and boxes we saw him with. The people had ordered the merchandise, and he was delivering it. The ones who hadn't prepaid were paying him at the time of delivery. Since this area is a big music lovers' paradise, it all makes sense. There are a lot of concerts on the beach and a lot of small music venues, and all of the restaurants seem to have live music."

Roberta added, "He actually has a website and sells a lot of his stuff on it, but he did sell it to local folks also. They had just had a big festival here, and he was selling a lot of it right now. I also asked if he knew what was going on at the shack behind the Seaside Corporation. David told me that a bunch of guys play poker there every week. He said he had never gone because they bet big money. He said all of his money was in his business."

Kea said, "We need to find out who these gamblers are. There may be a murderer among those folks."

We ate lunch, and I went back to baking. I made the frosting for the cake. I put a layer of cake on the platter; I punched holes in the cake, and poured some cream of coconut in the holes, slid the key lime pie onto the bottom layer, and then put the top cake layer on. The frosting came next, and then I patted on the toasted coconut. Now it was time for it to set up in the refrigerator, and then I was going to bribe my way into some homes by trading slices of cake for information.

When I told the other Salteens my plans for bribing people with my cake, they teased me. Jackie said, "You should give them some of the gifts you've received at previous volunteer Christmas events instead of the cake. We want all of the cake."

It was a standing joke that I always got the booby prize at every Christmas event we had. In past years, I had received vibrating pig feet, armadillo slippers, a reindeer head, and a thong! I didn't know how I managed to do this every year. I didn't know if it was bad luck or if they had all conspired against me to make sure I got it. I went off in a huff, but they knew I also thought it was funny.

I replied to Jackie with a retort, "You should plan the events at Christmas from now on so I will get acceptable gifts." A gag gift

Kea gave Otis was an autographed picture of all of us. She told him that since he loved autographed pictures of celebrities, she knew he would love that picture. We had a big laugh over that one.

Before we left for the afternoon, we set up the vision board in my bedroom, listing things we did know and things we didn't. On the side of the things we did know were the following:

- A creep named Art drives a blue van.
- Harriet Shelton was murdered.
- James Shelton is her husband.
- A lady named Sandra is her sister, and Oliver Garrison is her brother.
- Oliver delivers oil and works at the shop.
- Oliver is not the murderer, but he may be able to help with who did it.
- John Davis works at the shop and makes concert memorabilia.
- Matthew Hutzler is Harriet's boss and owns a lot of real estate in the area.
- William Shelton is an oil truck driver.
- Big-stakes gambling goes on in the shack behind the Seaside Corporation.
- The knife and the rest of Harriet's body were found at the service station.

What we didn't know included the following:

- If James, Matthew, John, and William have alibis (that would be a hard one until the coroner pinpoints a time and day of death, which may be impossible), who is involved in the gambling?

- Who is this Art guy?
- What was William doing driving the oil truck at night?
- Is there a connection between the Seaside Corporation and the Seaside Oil Company other than David buying the service station?
- Who is Sandra? We know she is Harriet's sister, but we haven't dug into her background.

We used up most of the sticky notes. The most important notes were on the side of things we didn't know.

Chapter 17

I cut up all the pieces of cake, put them on individual plates, and wrapped them up. Before we left to do some more sleuthing, Roberta, in all her infinite wisdom, knew I was nervous and edgy. She took me in her arms, looked me in the eyes, and said, "Don't worry. Don't scurry. Just twinkle. Just be who you are."

We figured out who we were going to visit. Lucy looked up all the unknown addresses, and the rest of the afternoon, we spent going to different places and passing out pieces of cake. It seemed to soften the hearts of some of the folks, particularly Harriet's sister, Sandra Anderson.

We drove up to Sandra's house and were amazed. She had one of the beautiful beach homes we loved. We were wondering what she and her husband did for a living to be able to afford such a nice place. We also wondered if a butler would answer the door. I said, "I don't know if I should go in. She really got mad at me for asking the drug question at the funeral home. I realize I lacked tact at the time, but I was upset."

Jackie said, "The worst thing that can happen is she will slam the door in our faces. Come on." I went rather slowly, following everyone, and kind of hid behind them when they rang the doorbell. The door opened.

"Hi," Roberta said. "We just wanted to come by and tell you that we are thinking about you, and we wanted to bring you some cake. We are so sorry if we upset you, but we were upset also. Sometimes things don't come out of your mouth right when you are distraught."

"I want to apologize to all of you for getting upset with you at the funeral home. My feelings were raw at the time. I understand now why you all desperately wanted answers to the murder. I am so mad right now that I want it just as bad you do. I heard you were asking questions around town. Have you found out anything useful to help with the case?"

"Not a lot," Roberta said. "We don't know how you feel about David's arrest, but we don't feel that he is guilty. Can you think of anything that can help us?"

"I agree. There is no way that he did this. He has always loved our whole family, and he loved Harriet at one time when they were dating. Ollie hung out with some scary characters when he was doing drugs. I wonder if it is somebody we don't even know although that doesn't explain why they would kill Harriet."

We saw somebody moving around in the background, then what to our wondering eyes should appear but the creepy politician we didn't want to come near. Sandra said, "Honey, look what these nice ladies brought us—some delicious cake slices." George and

Sandra were married! Sandra said, "This is my husband, George. I am so proud of him. He is running for the Senate right now, so he is really busy."

I managed to say, "We are lucky that we caught him here then."

George came up, put his arm around Sandra and nuzzled her. He said, "The death of Harriet is something my dear wife and I disagree on. I think it was David. A murderer is always who you least expect it to be. All of the evidence is right there at his work, so it has to be him. They found the murder weapon and the body parts in acid in the oil truck on his property."

I said, "That is true. It does seem to point to him. We're not convinced though. It was so lovely to see you again. We have to go."

We all thanked them and left. Roberta explained after we got in the car, "Sandra is going through the five different stages of grief. She was in denial when we saw her at the funeral home. Now she is in the anger phase. The next stages are bargaining, depression, and acceptance. I really wanted to tell her that I would do everything in my power to find out who did this, but I'm new to being a detective, so I knew I couldn't make any promises."

I said, "I did find it strange that George seemed to know things I would assume only the police would know. I am going to ask Zach if a lot of people in town know the location of where the knife was found and that the rest of Harriet's body was found in the oil truck with acid. I'm sure the mayor could possibly find out things because of his position in the town."

We went by the Seaside Shop to give Oliver a slice of cake. He was the only one there, and the pot odor was gone. He seemed to appreciate the thought. Jackie asked, "We brought a piece of cake for your coworker. Where is he?"

"I wish I knew. He didn't show up to work today. I have called, but there is no answer. I am supposed to go to my other job. I guess I'll have to call Seaside Corporation and tell them to get Billy to deliver in my place because I can't shut the doors of the shop."

We left the shop and decided our next plan of action was to find John Davis from the Seaside Shop, keep a lookout for the oil truck, and follow it if it left the service station again.

We also went by the funeral home, which was very close to our apartment. I wanted to give Ralph a piece of cake. We talked for a while. We told him we couldn't rest or go home until we knew who did this to poor Harriet. He was behind us all the way. I got some very skeptical looks from the Salteens when I said, "Ralph, I know this might seem strange, but if we need to borrow a car, can we use the hearse if it is not being used by the funeral home? We need something big enough for all of us, and we would only use it for a few minutes if an emergency arose."

"Of course, let me show you how to get a key."

I looked at my friends and winked. "Ralph, you don't know how much I appreciate this. I doubt we will use it, but it is nice to know it is here if we need it."

We left, and the Salteens couldn't wait to hear my explanation after leaving the funeral home. "What in the world are you borrowing a hearse for?" Jackie asked.

"So you can drive a sleek, cool car." Everyone laughed and waited for the explanation. "Moonshiners used hearses to transport their product. The federal agents would never suspect that car of hauling moonshine. We are going to use it to follow the oil truck so they won't suspect us."

"That is a great idea," Kea said.

Chapter 18

The next morning, we sat at the beach. Zach came down and talked to us. He asked why we were still there. We evaded the question by changing the subject. I said, "Would you like some of my prize-winning toasted coconut cake with a key lime pie layer?"

I could tell he wasn't falling for it, but he gladly accepted my offer. I was glad the vision board was in my bedroom so he couldn't see what we were really up to. Zach and I went back to the apartment, and I gave him a slice of cake to go. I asked, "Is it public knowledge that the murder weapon and the body parts in the oil truck were found at Seaside Oil Company?"

Zach said, "No, it is not, but as small as this area is, I'm sure the word might get out."

I asked, "Is there anything else you can tell me that would help us find who the murderer is?"

Zach said, "Please stop! I am afraid for you." He had a sad look on his face and left.

I didn't go back out to the beach because it was really hot. The rest of the Salteens came in, and we had lunch. After we ate, I suggested that we call the Seaside Shop and see if John was there so we could take him a piece of cake. Kea said, "Since you are the actress in the group, you need to call him and think up a reason to talk to him."

I changed my voice to an English accent, made the call, and asked to speak to John. Oliver didn't answer the phone. It was a woman, and she said John no longer worked there. "I wonder what happened," Roberta said. "Let's take a piece of cake to him at his house, and maybe he will tell us."

We went to his place. Lucy said, "He must be home since his car is here. We opened the car doors and immediately felt this ominous feeling.

Kea said, "I smell death."

"Oh no, don't say that!" Jackie exclaimed. That didn't sound good, so we slowly walked to the door and knocked.

We all looked at each other, because then we could all smell the horrible odor. Jackie said, "What is that odor?"

Lucy said. "I think it's a dead body."

I said, "What should we do? Should we call the police even though we don't know for sure?"

Roberta said, "Let's look in the front window. There are no curtains."

Kea said, "Can we get in trouble for that?"

I said, "I don't know, but if we see something, then we will know whether we need to call the police or not. I am going to try the door first." I went to the car and got out the gloves from my backpack. I tried to turn the door handle. "It is locked, so we need to look in a window."

We peeked in the front window and saw a crumpled mass sprawled on the floor. It was a man's body. His arm was all purple with a cord tied around it. There was blood coming out of his nose. His face was a putty color. It was John Davis.

Jackie started doing dry heaves. Roberta took her away from all of it across the street. We all started getting hysterical.

"This is not going to look good if we keep finding dead people. We are going to be the next suspects!" Kea said. I was beginning to feel the same way, but we had to call Zach.

He answered the phone immediately. "I loved that cake. Will you make me another one except this time I want a whole cake?"

I said, "After you hear what I have to say, you may not be able to keep that cake down."

"Oh no. What have you done now?" he asked.

I explained to him what we had discovered.

He said, "Is it John Davis?"

I said, "It looks like him to me."

He said, "Don't go anywhere!"

We sat on the steps and waited for the police to come. I said to my friends, "I am sorry that I keep getting you all into a mess. I can't believe this is happening."

Kea said, "Do you think they will suspect us?"

Lucy explained, "Not in this case. That looked like a drug overdose to me. There is no way that they can pin that on us. I just want us all to keep it together until we get back to the apartment." Then we heard the sirens and knew the police were just around the corner.

The officers broke into the house since the door was locked and checked the body's pulse. John Davis was dead. By then, we were all crying because we were afraid of what was going to happen next, and we couldn't take seeing any more dead people. We knew we hadn't done anything wrong, but it seemed like we had a black cloud hovering over us. Zach realized how upset we were. We told him we didn't know anything about his death. We only wanted to pass out cake to people we had met while we were here. He accepted that explanation though I'm not sure he believed it.

The next day Zach called and told us John had died of a drug overdose. I started crying and said, "This is particularly upsetting to me. Although I don't know the circumstances of John's death, I have known many people who have struggled with some sort of addiction. My son is a drug counselor, and he says we have made it much easier to get high than to get help. He stays so busy and is so frustrated at the insufficient access to treatment in the United States. More people die of drug overdoses than vehicle crashes and gun deaths combined. My son has been around more people who have died than I have, and I'm an old woman. He said that the only thing you can compare the drug overdose epidemic to is war.

"John is probably not near any family as far as we know since he is from Texas. This young man was somebody's son, and regardless of the choices he made, I am going to grieve for him. I just hope the police will find somebody who loved him soon. Right now, I don't trust anybody until this mess is cleared up. The only two innocent people right now, besides us, are Harriet and John. Now I am going to my room and cry an ugly cry."

Chapter 19

We all called our families at night to catch up on the news at home. After our phone calls, we gathered in the living room and shared other news such as who had died, who had a baby, who was sick, and who had committed a crime. I had done a face-to-face call with my dog. I really missed her a lot. We had been through a lot, and several of our family members wanted to come down and be with us. We discouraged this because it was getting too dangerous. We called Otis and caught him up on the details. He was horrified to hear everything. We had a question for him. If we caught the murderer, did he want his or her autograph?

The next thing on our agenda was to see where Billy Shelton took the oil truck at night. It may have just been a one-time deal, and he might not ever do it again, but we wanted to be ready just in case it happened again.

We couldn't go anywhere at night now because we had to keep a lookout for the oil truck. I was thinking we would probably hear it, but I didn't want to take a chance of missing it, so we decided to watch for it. We turned what we called the "lookout chair" around and could see the station from our front balcony. We all sat out there and took turns being in the lookout chair. We would stay up as late as we could.

We waited for two nights. Finally, on the third night, we saw it parked at the gas station. We hurriedly walked to the funeral home and got the hearse.

We brought it back to the apartment and waited to see whether Billy took off in the oil truck. After about an hour, we heard the oil truck motor being turned on. It was time for us to go. We followed him for about an hour.

He finally slowed down and pulled over to the side, parking perpendicular to a fence. We saw another car parked at the fence, so we turned before we got there and parked out of sight behind a grove of trees. We turned around in case we had to make a quick getaway. Jackie, our getaway driver, said, "This hearse isn't as easy to turn around as my little convertible."

We walked back to the fence on the opposite side of where the car and oil truck were parked, closer to where the hearse was hidden.

We were far enough away from them that I could talk a little above a whisper. I said, "I know exactly where we are! We are at an oil terminal. My daddy owned an oil tanker truck before he retired. He would get up at four in the morning, drive two hours, get that tanker filled up, and bring the fuel back to put in large, storage tanks at the back of his service station. He supplied people and other businesses with gas and oil. He had a smaller tank truck to deliver to homes for heating and tobacco barns for curing tobacco.

He would also get gas to use at the service station he owned. He took the fuel to marinas on a lake and smaller gas stations in our area. When he got really busy, my mama, who was a tomboy, would deliver oil to different places.

"I used to ride with my daddy sometimes in the summer when I was out of school. Once he took me across this dirt road, and beneath us was a dam they were building for hydroelectricity. He provided fuel for the electric company. There was a diving bell going down next to the dam as water was filling up the area. The people let my daddy go down in that diving bell to see the dam underwater."

Jackie interrupted, "Look! Billy is climbing the fence around the oil terminal."

Kea said, "He is pulling a long hose from the truck through the fence and attaching it to something by the huge tank."

I said, "He must have his own key to cut on the gas at the terminal. Why is he doing it like this?"

Roberta said, "He must be stealing gas!"

Suddenly, I heard what sounded like a seagull with laryngitis. I told the other girls to run for their lives back to the car. We all took off. We saw Billy run toward the oil truck. We heard the oil truck crank up its motor.

We got in the hearse. I told Jackie, our getaway driver, to gun it. As we drove by the terminal, I told her to put her hand on the bottom of her face, and I told everybody else to duck. Nobody there even followed us. I was grateful that they probably thought the hearse wasn't a getaway car. As we were going back to the beach, Jackie asked, "What just happened back there?"

I said, "Moonshiners would have a lookout a lot of times when they were working on their product. The lookout would howl like a coyote or hoot like an owl to warn them if any feds were coming. When I heard the noise that sounded like it could be a seagull—but I knew it wasn't really a seagull—I knew it was time for us to get out of there. The person who drove that car by the fence must have been the lookout. I don't know if he saw us or heard us. It could have even been someone else, but I didn't want to take any chances."

Jackie said, "Why did I have to hide the bottom of my face with my hand?"

I replied, "That is the 'moonshine howdy.' Whenever you didn't want someone to recognize you in a vehicle, particularly if you were transporting your moonshine, that was what you did. The only things the other folks could see were your eyes, so they had no idea who you were."

The Salteens were silent on the way back to the funeral home with the hearse. We rode by the Seaside Corporation. Roberta said, "Look! There's George and some woman getting out of a car and going to the shack!" We all quickly craned our necks, trying to sneak a peek.

Lucy said, "That does not look like Sandra. They must be gambling tonight."

I said, "Investigating the gambling is for another night. At least we know William Shelton is probably stealing gas. Now we need to find out why."

We took the hearse back to the funeral home, and then we cautiously walked back to the apartment. I looked out of the tall windows in the living room to a black-and-white picture. The waves were preparing to wash up some shells for the early-morning beach walkers to discover. All I saw was an ebony sky with white-crested waves. How could something so beautiful be in front of me with something so ugly somewhere behind me?

Chapter 20

It didn't take long for us to figure out what to do next the following morning. Sandra called. "Shirley Ann, Ollie got beat up last night. I have already lost my sister. I can't lose my brother, too. He won't talk to the police at all. Can you go to the hospital and talk to him? Maybe he will talk to you. George is staying home with me, because he is scared for my safety right now."

We packed into the car after breakfast and went to the hospital. Ollie looked like someone from a horror movie. His eyes were swollen shut, and we were sure he couldn't see a thing out of them. Bloody spit drooled from his slack jaws. His nose was smashed. One arm was in a cast, so it must have been broken, and the big purple welts on the rest of his body would eventually turn shades of blue, green, yellow, and black.

Jackie asked him, "Who did this horrible thing?"

He said, "I won't say because I am afraid it will happen to someone else that I love."

I said, "The police will help if you help them."

He replied, "These people are too brutal and have gotten by with this sort of thing for years. I can't tell the police."

I said, "Can you answer one question that shouldn't have anything to do with you getting beaten up?"

He said, "What's that?"

"Do you know someone named Art?" I asked.

He replied, "Yes. That is John Davis's brother, Art Davis. John worked with me at the Seaside Shop, but now he's dead." We all acted surprised at the news like we hadn't seen his dead body.

He continued, "John did that to himself. He was an addict, I think. All I know is Art is one of the poker card players in the shed behind Seaside Corporation."

Roberta asked, "Who else plays poker?"

He said, "My brother-in-law, George, and some of his friends. You have to be wealthy to play the kind of game they play."

Kea said, "We are all sorry that this happened to you. Please call us if you need anything and please tell the police."

When we got back to the car, Lucy said, "Maybe someone in the poker gang plays a part in what is going on. We guessed right when we saw George at the shack. He was going to play poker. We have to figure out how to find the person or persons causing all of this before someone else gets hurt. Oliver looked terrible."

When we got home, Lucy looked Art up on her computer now that she also knew his last name. She said, "Art has quite a rap sheet. He has had numerous arrests. He has an assault conviction, possession of drugs, distribution of drugs, and other minor arrests."

We looked at his mug shot. Roberta said facetiously, "He sounds like such a nice guy."

Jackie said, "Hey, now I know where we saw Art. Remember the guy trying to eavesdrop on us when we were talking to David at the service station? Kea, that is probably why you smelled gas in the van. He had been there that day, and David may have worked on his vehicle." We all nodded in agreement.

Kea said, "It's a rainy day, so we can't go to the beach. What do you want to do?"

Jackie said, "We could go shopping."

I said, "I want to cook."

Jackie, Kea, and Roberta went shopping. Lucy wanted to stay and read. I went to the grocery store. This time I wanted to make a carrot cake with a cheesecake layer. We bought the ingredients and came back to the apartment.

First, I made the crust in the springform pan, cooked it, and allowed it to cool. Then I made the cheesecake and put it in the refrigerator. I shredded the carrots, poured them in the cake batter, and cooked the cake layers. After the cake layers were cooled off, I put one cake layer on the cake platter; then I slid the cheesecake off the springform pan. Lastly, I put the top layer on the cheesecake. I had to cut off some of the cheesecake because it oozed out and was bigger than the cake layers. Those cheesecake pieces would be good for snacking on later. I put the cake all together and frosted it with butternut cream icing.

The other Salteens came in as I was putting the last of the frosting on the cake. There was a knock at our door. It was a man we had never seen before. "Hi, my name is Ned Amos. I am part of the FBI task force participating in Project Opioid, which is part of a cooperation among federal, state, and local law enforcement agencies and the government of Mexico. We are trying to find out what part of the Mexican cartel is running drugs up our way. Zach and I think it would be in your best interest to go home as soon as possible, because this could get ugly before it's over with. These people are very dangerous."

I asked him whether he wanted a piece of cake. The Salteens all looked at me because they knew bribery was about to start. I asked him, "Do you have any idea who would be involved locally?"

He wouldn't say. I asked several other questions and got nowhere. As he was leaving, he thanked me for the cake and said, "We do have reason to believe that the deaths of Harriet Shelton and John Davis and the brutal beating of Oliver Garrison are all related, so we need to protect all of you. Go home. Be safe."

Kea said, "He didn't have to tell me twice."

I said, "We'll leave first thing in the morning. It's late to be heading out now. We'll be fresh in the morning."

Chapter 21

We started to pack up our things. We called our families and told them we were coming home. We spent the rest of the afternoon and evening telling everyone we had met goodbye and giving them a piece of cake. One piece of good news was that David had been released from jail. We went by his mom's house to tell him goodbye. His mom answered the door. When she found out who we were, she hugged all of us. She said, "Thank you so much for trying to help my baby boy."

Lucy said, "We knew he didn't murder anybody."

We could tell David was exhausted, so we didn't learn a lot of the details. He said, "I want to thank you for all you did. They knew that I couldn't have beat up Ollie since I was in jail so they couldn't pin that one on me." We assumed that they would have to have some proof that he didn't commit the murder for him to be released. We gave David and his mom some cake and bid them farewell.

I lay down in the bed that night and wished I could figure out all the pieces of the puzzle. I knew it was right in front of me. I felt like maybe there was a connection between Art and John coming here and living in Texas. Texas borders Mexico, which was where the cartel was from, but I didn't know how I would ever be able to discover all that. It was best for the big dogs of the FBI to get to the bottom of it. Besides, the situation was getting too dangerous. Hopefully, we had made enough connections so someone would let us know when the mystery was solved.

Chapter 22

The next morning the Salteens wanted to take a walk on the beach before we left. I had a few things to clean up in the kitchen. We had gotten really lax about leaving the door open to the apartment, particularly when part of the gang was at the beach. I didn't think anything about it when someone came through the door.

I was in the kitchen cleaning with my back turned, and I said, "Did you have fun on your final walk?" Suddenly someone grabbed me as I turned around. Thick fingers grabbed my arm and hair and threw me onto the floor. I recognized the political monster in front of me. The upset, fearful, and troubled look on his face made the situation all too real. This sick person had been in our lives.

He put a knee on my chest, gagged me, and tied my hands with a rope. He picked me up and dragged me to the door. He opened it, and there was no one around to help me. I couldn't scream anyway with this gag on. What did he want with me?

He opened a car trunk and heaved me in, slamming my head on the trunk floor. Sweat dripped down my forehead, and I fought a wave of nausea. He closed the trunk door.

A dizzy sensation crept up my body, making me feel helpless. I had to think fast. What could I do to save myself? I knew if I panicked, I would freak, flail, freeze, and be easy meat for this beast.

I had read that you should kick the lights out if you ever got trapped inside a trunk. I couldn't get enough leverage to kick since I was so afraid, and it was dark in the trunk. I felt around in the car. There were boxes of what smelled like paper money, but I wasn't sure. I didn't have Kea's nose.

I finally found the back of the car. I knew the first thing I had to do was calm myself down. Reeling from the pain in my head, I struggled to get in a position to kick the lights out of the trunk. I took a few deep breaths. I sucked in a final breath, pulled my abdominal muscles to my back, and kicked with all my might. Aha! One of the lights broke. I just prayed that the monster driving hadn't heard anything.

I had to leave a Hansel and Gretel trail. I got into one of those boxes and started throwing the paper from it out the hole I had made when I kicked the light out. It was the shape of money, but I still wasn't sure what it was. I didn't want to throw out too much or the driver might see it, but I wanted enough that eventually someone would notice, especially if it was real money.

We rode in the car for what seemed forever. The car finally stopped. The trunk was flung open. The driver was furious at me when he saw that I had kicked out his tail light and gotten into the box. He said, "So you thought you would be smart and kick out my taillight and get into my money? Well, it didn't do you a bit of good, because there's nobody around to see us."

A dead, almost inhuman look came on his face, and he slammed me onto the trunk floor as hard as he could, smacking my head hard and making me see stars. I put my tied hands up to protect myself, and he bit my finger, opening the flesh nearly to the bone. I started bleeding. Blood poured down my face, obscuring my vision.

"Now I'm going to kill you!" he said. I was blindfolded and grabbed again. The pressure in my head was bursting. I was going to die! The feeling of death is more fearful than anything. I began to remember all the things I wanted to do with my life, but life was becoming fruitless.

I heard his heavy boots walking as he dragged me along. I was heaved onto another area. I could hear the waves, so I knew we were near the ocean. The floor rocked. I was on a boat. The boat's motor started with a deep purr.

My mind went from freaking out to being very calm. I prepared myself to die. I thought about what the headlines in tomorrow's paper would be and what people would say at my funeral. I thought about the Salteens and prayed that none of them would get hurt, because this was my fault for getting them into this mess. I was angry at myself for putting them in danger.

I was having a huge information blast at this moment. My whole life flashed in front of me. I wanted things to stop, fast-forward, or even better, I wanted to realize it was a nightmare. I realized how thin the gap was between life and death. I kept thinking about my family and whether I would ever see them again. I wanted to see my granddaughter grow up. I thought about how my ninety-year-old daddy was going to feel about all this.

We went out for a short distance, and he lifted me up and threw me overboard. I plunged into the water while squeezing my eyes shut. I was sinking, and no one could save me now. I was alone.

My body did whatever it could to save my life. I kicked with all my might, because he hadn't tied my legs up. The water was cold, but oddly, there was something about it I liked.

I found myself in a place that was soft and glowing white. I could feel deep love pouring into me. I also knew and understood that everything in my world was connected and meant to be. There was a reason for every person I had ever met and everything I had ever experienced, both good and bad. I wanted to tell my family goodbye. This wasn't how I wanted to die. My lungs began to fill, so I had to give up. I was going to be with my mama and grandmother.

Suddenly, I felt a hand grab me. We quickly swam to the top, and I gasped for air. By then, the salt water had made the gag fall off. Just then, I heard a voice.

"Shirley Ann, Shirley Ann! Wake up!" It was Zach. He was my hero.

Then I think I passed out. I don't remember anything. Then Zach started trying to resuscitate me, and I started vomiting. I do remember that. It took a few seconds for my throbbing head to clear. Then I remembered. I had to force my eyes open.

"Follow the guy on the boat," I cried. "Get who did this to me!" Then I began to shake from shock. The ambulance came and took me to the hospital.

I initially had some bruising and sharp head pain, which gave way to a dull ache. My chest burned. I had a cough and shallow breath from almost drowning. The hospital staff told me that people could experience a range of physical, mental, emotional, and behavioral reactions after what I had been through. It was normal to have strong reactions following a traumatic event, but they should dissipate after a few weeks.

I had to stay in the hospital for a few days. I insisted that the Salteens go on home; someone from my family would pick me up and take me home when I was released. But they wouldn't go. The Salteens told me I had bluish skin at first. Lucy and Roberta had medical backgrounds and were afraid I would have brain damage from the lack of oxygen.

They took turns with me during my stay at the hospital.

Zach came to see me while Kea and I were having fun joking around with the nursing staff. We had just taken a picture with Otis in the hospital bed with me.

Zach had a lot to tell us. "I came to tell all of you goodbye the morning you were hogtied and dumped over the boat. Ned Amos told me that he had talked all of you into going home. I saw George Anderson's car speed away from the apartment and noticed that your door had been left open, so I decided to follow him.

"I was off duty and not in my police car. Then the rear light of his car was kicked out, and money started flying out of the hole. I called for police backup, but before they could get there, the car started slowing down where people dock their boats in the intercoastal waterway. I kept on going down the road and parked.

"I saw George go to his trunk and watched him drag you to his boat. He revved up his boat engine and left the pier, so I ran to a local owner's boat because I knew where he kept his keys. In the meantime, I called the coast guard. By then, George knew someone was following him. I saw him dump something in the water and take off toward the ocean. I stopped and got you out of the water and called for an ambulance. The coast guard found and arrested George Anderson."

The rest of the Salteens walked into my hospital room. Kea said, "What about that crazy-driving Art guy? What does he have to do with all of this?"

Zach said, "Ned Amos was here to do surveillance on him. Art Davis was sent here by the Mexican cartel to launder money and distribute drugs. He was at the service station when you were asking David questions about going dancing, and he got the idea to be the hired driver. He got nervous when y'all were asking questions around town, so he thought he might be able to find out what you knew. He also sent those guys down to the beach to eavesdrop on all of you. Ned Amos arrested him on several charges."

Roberta said, "I remember him being at the service station and listening to us. We were told that Art and John are related. Is that true?"

"Yes," Zach replied. "They were brothers. John came here for a new life that was clean and legal. He smoked pot occasionally. He got so upset when he heard Harriet was murdered that he deliberately overdosed. He felt like the death was connected in some way to the cartel. The sad part was that her death had nothing to do with the cartel. Art started crying when he told me that his brother had left him a voice message before he took his own life."

Lucy said, "Why was Harriet killed?"

Zach said, "Harriet caught George Anderson with a woman in the shack. He killed her because he was afraid she would tell someone. If she did, he would lose his chances of winning the Senate race."

Jackie asked, "Was there a connection between George Anderson and Art Davis?"

"George was helping him to launder the drug money through the high-stakes poker games at the shack behind the Seaside Corporation. He knew George had gotten Harriet to meet him at the beach to talk about what she had seen at the shack. That's when he killed her. Art helped George try to frame David for Harriet's murder by putting the murder weapon and the body parts at the service station. He accidentally left the hand on the beach. Art squealed on George Anderson, but he wouldn't say who his connection was in the Mexican cartel."

"Why did Ollie get beat up?" I asked.

"When Ollie approached George about his suspicions, George beat him up and told him the rest of his family was going to be in real danger if he didn't keep his mouth shut. George was arrested for murder, multiple assault and battery incidents, the kidnapping of an individual, and the attempted drowning of an individual. There went his political career. Art was charged with aiding and abetting in a murder."

Lucy said, "I feel so bad for Sandra. She lost her sister. Then she finds out the man that she loved killed her. I can't imagine what she is feeling right now."

I said, "What happened to William Shelton?"

"Billy Shelton was arrested for theft at the oil terminal. Both he and Ollie had participated in the high-stakes poker games. Only Ollie paid off his debt the honest way by working two jobs. Billy decided to steal gas and get money for it to pay off his debt."

Ned Amos was on the news that night. "I am Ned Amos, a part of the FBI drug task force. With these arrests, a major fentanyl distribution organization had been dismantled. I'd like to thank the entire law enforcement team that worked so hard on this case. This case demonstrates cooperation and teamwork at their best. Today's arrests are the result of an aggressive strategy to target those who allegedly profit off the distribution of counterfeit pills laced with deadly amounts of fentanyl. We will continue to investigate others who may be responsible for distributing illegal drugs throughout our communities in an effort to save lives."

I left the hospital after two days. When I arrived at the apartment, it seemed like the whole town was there to greet me. The Salteens, Sandra, and a few others had planned a big welcome-back party for me. There was a big sign that said, "WELCOME HOME!" And of course, they had brought cake and moonshine.

David from the Seaside Oil Company gave us all a big hug. He said, "If it hadn't been for the Salteens, I might still be in jail. You don't know how much I appreciate what you did. Please be careful on your next adventure."

People asked whether I had anything to say about what had happened. I looked at the Salteens, and the tears started flowing. I said, "Victor Hugo once said, 'Music expresses that which cannot be put into words and that which cannot remain silent.' I'm looking at people who I became friends with at first through music and then through salt. Friends need not agree about everything. Politically, friends may be on opposite sides. They just have to perceive that there's something important we all have in common. Salt was widely and variably used as a symbol and sacred sign in ancient Israel and in many cultures. It is even mentioned that the eating of salt is a sign of friendship. Loving friends is something we do because we want to. You don't have the day-to-day burdens weighing you down with them like sharing a bedroom or bathroom, and you don't have to depend on any one person for your needs. You can have as many as you want, and they can have all sorts of qualities. It always helps to have people we love beside us when we have to do difficult things in life."

Before everyone left, we all had a moonshine toast with Otis in the picture one last time.

We finished packing up, and all the people who talked to us said we could come back anytime and stay free of charge. I wasn't too sure any of us would come back to Seaside Beach, but we had gained some new friends. We got in our cars, and as we drove out of the beach area, people who hadn't been able to attend the party came out of their shops and other places of business and waved goodbye.

I will always have my Salteens.

People asked whether I had anything to say about what had happened [illegible] the band and [illegible] started [illegible]. I said [illegible] once said, "Music expresses that which cannot be put into words and that which cannot remain silent." I'm fortunate [illegible] people who became friends [illegible] through [illegible] through [illegible]. Friends need not agree about everything [illegible] friends may be on opposite sides. They just have to [illegible] share something [illegible] all have in common [illegible] and [illegible] in Israel and [illegible]. [illegible] even mentioned that [illegible] of all is [illegible] of friendship. Losing friends is something we [illegible] to. [illegible] don't [illegible] the day [illegible] with them [illegible] on any [illegible] as many [illegible] they can [illegible] acquaintances. It always helps to have people who love us [illegible] difficult things [illegible].

A good friend is a connection to life—a tie
to the past, a road to the future.
—Lois Wyse

Before [illegible] we all [illegible] the toast [illegible] the picture ended.

We finished packing up and all the people who [illegible] so we could [illegible] and stay [illegible] and [illegible] of us would come back to Seaside Beach, but we had gained some new friends. We got in our cars, and as we drove out of the [illegible] area, people who had [illegible] to attend the party came out [illegible] and waved [illegible].

I will always love my [illegible].

#Acknowledgments

To my parents: Thank you for your many sacrifices to make a better world for me. You always made me believe I could do anything. I love you.

To my son and his family: Always remember that there is nothing as great as a mother's love. I love you.

To my husband: You are my best friend and partner in life. I love you.

To my Salteens: You are my inspiration. I know there will be shenanigans involved when we get together. I love you.

Saltines
2019

Saltines 2020 Pandemic

Dollywood